The Steve Machine

a novel by Mike Hoolboom

Coach House Books
Toronto

first edition

 Canada Council   Conseil des Arts   ONTARIO ARTS COUNCIL   Canadä
for the Arts   du Canada   CONSEIL DES ARTS DE L'ONTARIO

Published with the generous assistance of the Canada Council for
the Arts and the Ontario Arts Council. Coach House Books also
acknowledges the support of the Government of Ontario through
the Ontario Book Publishing Tax Credit and the Government of
Canada through the Book Publishing Industry Development
Program.

All characters in *The Steve Machine* are fictional. There exists a real
Steve Reinke, who shares some qualities with the Steve Reinke in
this book, but this is *by no means* an accurate depiction of him, nor
is it intended to be.

LIBRARY AND ARCHIVES CANADA CATALOGUING IN PUBLICATION

Hoolboom, Michael
    The Steve machine / Mike Hoolboom.

ISBN 978-1-55245-202-8

    1. Reinke, Steve, 1963- --Fiction. I. Title.

PS8615.O515S74 2008   C813'.6   C2008-905272-2

'The most complicated machines
are made only with words.'
– Jacques Lacan

*O*ne morning I picked up a book, I can't remember which one, and as I read I began to hear a voice inside, as if it were speaking to me. Ever since, whenever I read, I hear that same voice. It took me many years and many more books before I discovered the owner of those summery tones, and this volume is a record of that quest. But not only that. It is also a machine for producing this voice. When the book is finished, you will be able to hear what I hear: the voice of Steve Reinke. This may take some getting used to at first, but I want to reassure you that the transition is generally effortless. When it finally arrives, you will very likely ask yourself: how did I ever make it through a book without this accompaniment? How could I have waited so long? Every book is part of the library, and inside that library there is a voice already waiting for you. And you won't have to turn the last page of the last book before the promise of well-being and comfort issuing from that voice belongs to you.

You've come home.

He looked too young to tell anyone they were going to die. Too young to admit even the possibility of death, though he was a doctor, so maybe it came with the office. There was a sadness in this doctor's face that remained a stranger to him, and it kept him young. One day all that unhappiness would catch up to him and he'd grow old in an hour that lasted a hundred years.

'I'm afraid the results aren't good,' the doctor began, looking almost sad, like a fifteen-year-old doing Shakespeare. He was trying to look glum through the tube tan, his perfect tennis game, the annual sex vacation in Thailand, but it wasn't quite working. I felt myself filling with concern. I knew this couldn't be easy for him, especially not before lunch. It was hard to feel anything on an empty stomach, except maybe a longing for the award-winning ice cream they made downstairs. At least ice cream didn't smell. It would be torment having to lead the parade of the unwell while those fragrant compounds played through the office, offering forty-three kinds of heaven.

'We've run both tests, so there's not much doubt now. You're HIV-positive.'

I nodded, worried I wasn't managing the proper expression. HIV-positive? I felt the muscles in my face as a large pack of steel balls that needed to be coaxed and herded to form basic human responses. Only they seemed a little frozen, tired maybe, which made the poor man in front of me, this masquerade of a doctor, look extremely agitated. I don't know why, but this struck me as being funny all of a sudden, and I started laughing in a way I hadn't laughed for a long time. It was such a relief that even though I knew it was the wrong thing to do, even though I felt awful for this stranger sitting next to me, I couldn't stop.

I laughed on and on and then I realized I would have to leave. Sudbury wasn't big enough for news like this. It had offered me a steady diet of fax machines and eight-track tapes and pocket calculators, and when those were gone I chugalugged MTV, four-wheel drives and personal transport vehicles that wouldn't have looked out of place in the Normandy Invasion. And now AIDS. The doctor was telling me it was time to leave these dreams, this body, behind. He mumbled into his diploma and the stethoscope that hung uselessly around his neck. He could have given me pills for stress or anxiety, but he never mentioned it, maybe he was saving them for himself. I gave him my firmest goodbye grip, and his hand felt like it had been left out in the rain. Someone who looked just like me strode out the door with a whistle in his step. Begone, dull care.

What I needed above all was to feel strangers rushing past me. I wanted to look into faces that would stare right through mine. *I don't care.* That's what I hoped for most of all. *I don't know you.* Music to my shrinking ears. It was time to push on. The stairway delivered me to the front door where I could leave the dream of this doctor, this afternoon, behind. Dying. I was twenty-five years old and I was dying. Is that what he said?

When I got back to my basement bachelor, I pulled out a yellowing backpack from the closet and stuffed it up with shirts and underwear and a couple of books. Whatever. I was a week and a half late on the rent, but because I'd been such a model citizen, the landlady, who lived upstairs on a strict diet of 7-Up and Southern Comfort, had let it slide. Mrs. Waxley. Call me Doris, she said, but I didn't. Drank her Comfort sometimes in a room she liked to call her parlour, but after three or four she would always want to crank up the big-band swings and dance, and I wasn't much of a partner. Flat feet, I told her, and then she'd forget so I'd tell her again. She liked to talk about things coming up when she was my age more or less, and I warmed to see her like that, glowing with the Comfort and her once-upon-a-times. I left her a note that said I was going to Toronto because of some family questions and I wondered if she would remember that I didn't have a family, but that didn't seem too likely. Facts didn't tend to stick to her.

The pack wasn't nearly big enough to fit the collections of coasters and bottle caps and strangers' postcards I liked to pick up at the weekend flea markets, but even the crumbs I stowed seemed extravagant. I was going to miss the records, though. Some newbody would swap the lot of them for a twenty-spot at Handsome's Second Hand, too conveniently located a couple of blocks away. Let them have it, I guessed. I waited until it was dark, until I could hear Mrs. Waxley's heavy, Comfort-soaked steps trudge from the parlour to her bedroom, and the protesting squeal of mattress springs as she sank into them. The bus station was all the way across the map, but there was still plenty of time before the last out-of-towner pulled away.

I stepped out into the night breeze, which was fresher now that the Superstack blew our nickel-mine dandruff into more distant neighbourhoods. With every crack of the sidewalk I muttered, 'Goodbye. Goodbye. Goodbye,' until I forgot about it. NASA had sent a team of astronauts up here so they could get a feel for what it would be like on the moon, but that was a few years back, before people could keep a front lawn growing. I stopped at a red light, and then another, even though I was the only beating heart in the neighbourhood. As the light glowed green, I could feel a small spark go off in my chest, as if there were some tiny bedroom waiting there nestled between my liver and kidneys, all pink and plush and soft, and I could almost hear the door shut and feet padding across carpet. Princess retiring for the night.

In the space of five blocks I got so worn down I had to sit for a minute. It had been happening more and more lately. But I pushed the feeling away and pretended to continue walking to the bus station until it was there in front of me. I impersonated a ticket purchase, a man waiting on the seat, a person who enjoyed lineups. I was on the way.

Toronto. I'd been dreaming of the city ever since I had legs to take me there. It had a reassuring greyness, a suspicion of anything or anyone grown too large. Even the neon was pale. It seemed just the place to start counting down the days.

We rolled in before sunset, the stage set of buildings and emptied avenues waiting for a keyword to bring them around. The terminal had the same kicked-dog look of every bus depot in the world, so I picked up a paper and ran grease-pencil circles over every apartment listing I could afford. I palmed a roll of quarters and waited over bad coffee and some sugared deep-fry that even Tim Horton would have been embarrassed to call a doughnut before picking a spot in a cluster of public phones. Oh no, I didn't mind calling back at all. References? No, I didn't have any pets. The auditions had begun.

The building that got its hook into me was an eleven-floor high-rise with a room just large enough to stretch out in while offering a brilliant look across the water. Yes, Lake Ontario, the greatest of the Great Lakes, was clearly visible between the neighbouring condo lookouts, their three ivory teeth roaring into the clouds. My building was so noisy and cheap that I could hardly hear myself think: children were busy dragging the corpses of brand-name TVs and iThings and appliances still wearing bubble wrap up a stairwell that had been refurnished in black felt marker. There was a steady smell of bacon frying and the sound of large dogs shouting at smaller dogs. The men had quick little names like Kit or Sam or John, which they slid out of their mouths real fast and which would pass right on by if you weren't paying attention, while the women had names like Gwendolyn and Prahiti and Tojiku, as if they'd all graduated from the same college of polysyllabic indifference. They looked at you and their eyes said, *So what?* As soon as I moved in, I felt my mood improving. I was going to like it here.

'I'm not the landlord, I'm the super. I work for the management company,' said the round ball of a man who jiggled his way through the doors of my apartment. Roach spray and balding carpet. sos pads and Mr. Clean over everything. When I paid him in cash, he looked at me like we were finally playing on the same team and smiled. He folded the money into squares that grew smaller and smaller as he walked me across the vacancy.

What I really wanted was a plastic surgeon and a shop filled with every face in the world. I'd take one for workdays and another for weekends. Perhaps the one with blond curls to sleep inside. I couldn't help wondering if anyone would have the jam to pick out the face that looked exactly like the one they were already wearing.

'I don't expect we'll be seeing each other much,' he told me in a hoarse whisper stolen from a Charles Bronson movie as he handed me the keys. I stole glances at the shiny redheads he had inked over the knuckles of his hands. Whenever he moved his fingers it looked like their legs were kicking, which was a pretty neat trick for a homemade fountain-pen job. When he left, the door closed behind him by itself, fighting a last current of hallway exhaust until it gave in and the metal tongue found its mouth.

Light flickered off the condo towers and licked up the carpet in soft streaks. In a couple of hours the sky would go dark and my apartment along with it. I stretched out in the warm spot and looked at a hand that might have belonged to someone else. I was never big on change. Even adolescence had appeared in a reluctant fade of encroaching hair and lowered expectations. But the only way to survive this plague was to become someone else. I would let the illness ravage the body of the person I used to be, destroy it layer by layer until there was nothing left. I was determined to escape and give myself over to someone who could never be positive. I wanted to ride the whole wagon: the new me wouldn't even get colds or flus, he'd walk through infirm armies never needing a handkerchief, swim inside pus balls, vacation in leper colonies. A clean bill of health.

I started going to the gym at the local community centre, where the neighbourhood reconvened itself one muscle group at a time. Someone had donated a boom box to the room, so that the turbulence of our exertions would not be dealt to our neighbours. Although I could feel breakfast rising every time I approached the door, I was determined to embrace the radio's high-octane disc spinners and their noxious blend of sentimental corporate rock and millionaire rapolas. I strained beneath pegged iron blocks that had been hoisted only moments before without any apparent effort by teenage assassins who paused between reps to adjust their fingerless gloves. I tried to say yes. Yes to the tried-and-truisms that struggled out of the radio's electronic pacifier. Yes to the smiling self-regard the mirror held as we snuck a look or two at our new bodies. Was that a chest I saw growing there? The beginnings of an abdomen, perhaps not a six-pack, but a lonesome ripple crossing the wasteland? Oh yes, and more.

The first week after sign-up I went every day until I was approached by a silver-maned bear whose neck was so muscled he had to turn his entire torso to face his listeners. This gave him the appearance of an overgrown child's toy, and made conversation distracting. He told me I should take a day off to let my muscles heal up and I thanked him for the good word. When I got back in after a day's vacation I was so hungry to lift I would sometimes do back-to-back sets. It wasn't long before I realized the great, treasured secret of every workout hound in the city.

It wasn't the muscles after all, or the steadily accumulating progress of iron. The irresistible seduction lay in the fact that inside those mirrored walls, all thinking crawled to a halt. Every kind of worry took off in the face of the next lift, the closing abdominal crunch. Even though it might last only a minute or two, the endless trivia quiz of my waking life grew quiet at the sight of all that metal, and I felt myself growing lighter, hardly a body at all. The great escape had begun.

I had worked the mill back home, like most everyone else, and in between there had been a series of no-name jobs like painting houses and washing cars and even a stint as a security guard. But here in my new city I was determined to pick up a different plate. After I failed science two years in a row, my guidance counsellor, who we both knew was only a retired phys. ed. instructor, relented and allowed me to take a knot of secretarial courses. Hoping nobody would have enough game to check out-of-town referrals, I created a fine new employment past and signed on with Workforce, plumping for an office hire. Inside two weeks I was behind the desk at McCrearie's, a small insurance hive specializing in big-risk clients. My boss was hardly older than I was, only Johnson had never failed science. His position made him seem larger than he was, a hairless bowling pin with eye rings that sagged into a pair of defeated cheeks. He had an enormous desk he never sat behind, preferring quick, improvised runs up and down the hallway as he paced out his new concern. It seemed his brain worked only while he was on the move, so his secretary, meaning moi, was required to jostle behind him scribbling down his every smirk of genius.

In his company I heard the word *yes* turned into everything but dessert. It was dished as greeting, warning, sign-off and exclamation point. 'Yes?' he would say as he greeted me in the morning. He was already there, of course. I never saw him leave the office, not even to go for lunch. He preferred to be around 'the heat,' as he liked to call it, wearing his brown leather loafers down to the nubs of their tassels.

It became obvious, after the first couple of months, that Johnson had no time or inclination for what he sneeringly referred to as 'a private life.' Along with his correspondence, his endless filing requests and note takings, I booked appointments with his chiropractor and rowing team. But as my temp posture began to lean into something more permanent, I was asked to book liaisons with escorts. It was understood, of course, that if I breathed a word about it I would be shown the door.

My temp-worker status suited both of us too well. As soon as I left the office it was as if it had never happened. And I can't recall Johnson ever asking me a personal question, not even at the interview. When I met him for the first time he was standing at his desk behind a mountain of paper that he shuffled around for a few minutes before looking up at me. 'Yes?' he asked, as if that were a question. 'Yes?' I answered. 'Yes, are you serious, have you come here to work?' 'Yes,' I said, 'I would like that very much.' We made a point of never looking back.

From a Salvation Army remainder box I bought ten identical baby-blue T-shirts that screamed 'Ted's' across the chest, sleeves and neck. If Ted was going to spring for the merchandise then people were going to know about it. At the gym they started calling me Ted's and I loved that. Not Ted but Ted's.

I had worked my bench press up over twenty-five kilos and walked home that night looking forward to a TV dinner and then maybe dancing at Soccerdads. I liked wearing the T-shirts over there too, but no one had called me Ted's. Yet. A couple of blocks from home I ran into a front of lake breeze and felt suspended in the summer currents, which I could see approaching and receding like kite trails of warm and warmer. Each moment of skin dissolved into atoms turning, and when I looked out onto the strip of grass that followed the walk, I could see a thousand varieties of green in a single stem. My knees grew soft and I pushed my arms out in front of my face to keep it from hurting later. The ground fell, and then the trees and lake.

The sound of traffic like a warm blanket. I tried to turn over but my body was too far away to reach. There was one point left in the world, one small hole left for me to look through. It was green and soft and comfortable, so I settled into it and closed my eyes and went to sleep. I might have lain there for an hour or several days, but when I woke it was dark. I wiped the dust off my Ted's and saw my apartment waiting just ahead. A posse of small children ran up to cars stopped at the light and pointed their fingers at the drivers and shouted, 'Bang! You're dead,' and ran away laughing. I nodded as I stepped inside.

He seemed to inhabit his skin like an old couch, like it was something big and comfortable and well-worn, and he invited anyone in sight to roll around in it with him. His name was Niko and he was the most undiscriminating man I'd ever met. His charms lay scattered about him like spoiled buckshot, aimed at anything that moved. He was an egomaniac without an ego, a shameless bully who flattered anyone he thought was better than himself, which included almost everyone. He just wanted to be everyone's friend, kind of, which mostly meant he didn't have any friends at all.

The person I used to be wouldn't have noticed Niko if he were the last one standing on the island, but the new me, or at least the person I had begun releasing in one-arm dumbbell rows and wide-grip pull-downs, clamped onto Niko and wouldn't let up. With his help, I might lose any trace of the one giving way to illness. There would be no whim too grey, no service too low, that I wouldn't perform with a smile.

We met at the Speedomatic Laundry, which wasn't very matic and certainly wasn't speedy. Niko had staggered towards the door with a year's worth of clothing reruns straining out of a garbage bag that burst as he tried to ease it through the small broken entrance that seemed especially designed, like the Speedomatic itself, to discourage all comers. He cursed loudly and easily, in a language that turned out to be Greek, then cast about for assistance from the chattering classes. He was a small-boned twenty-something with a shock of black hair rising straight from his scalp, which gave him a permanently surprised expression. *Oh really?* his face seemed to say, even if he was bored, or turned on, or angry enough to put his fist through a window. Which he didn't do often, not anymore.

Niko wasn't from here, like just about everyone else. He had spent the years after high school wandering through nuclear test sites, just to be alone, he told me later, though I wondered what he was really after out there. Sometimes I thought I could still catch a glimpse of all that desert up inside him, though it might have been my projector running overtime.

I was beside him in a moment, stooping through the piles of thrift-store ware and hustler sweats that passed for Niko's wardrobe, bits of it plastered together with something that appeared suspiciously like chili. We bundled it in tidy piles by the nearest machine and came back for more, Niko pausing to direct the flow like he'd arranged the whole thing. Finally he turned to me and said, 'My service is on holidays, so here I am on a Friday night. What a nightmare. If you don't wash them right away, clothes expand in the bag, like peanuts. Don't you find?' I didn't find, but I wasn't about to let on. Because there was nothing about him that was sweet to the taste, I knew he was going to become my new best friend. My very own anti-madeleine. One look at him, and I would be able to forget everything.

'Do you work there?' Niko asked me, nodding at my chest.

'Where?'

'At Ted's,' he remarked in a voice that made clear he didn't care what my answer was.

'No, not yet,' I told him. 'I thought I'd buy the shirt and see how it felt.'

'Classic,' he replied, and promptly lost himself in the stop-and-start turn of the washer. It wasn't drugs that lent his eyes that midnight glow but good old-fashioned indifference. I was closing in.

Niko was always getting me to do things. Picking up lawn chairs, for instance, though there wasn't a lawn within five kilometres. 'But, Auden, you were going in that direction anyway, right?' When his apartment started taking on gas, I was first on the speed dial and replumbed the stove. 'You saved my life, Auden. I *swear* I was this close to lighting a cigarette.' His apartment was forever breaking down, and I always arrived with the same canned determination that propelled me to the gym. No matter how little I did, his face would stare back with gratitude and wonder, like he was looking at the pyramids or something. I didn't think there was that much thanks left in the world, and it all belonged to me. It made him appear almost human, and granted me a rare shine unmatched until I met Steve, but that didn't happen until after the orgy.

'I'm having a little get-together tonight,' Niko let on, trying for casual. Only he was almost whispering when he said it, so it sounded like he was trading state secrets.

'Oh yeah?'

'You should come. It's a bit of an o-r-g-y.'

Niko was the only one who ever called it that. He looked about seventy years old when he said it, and I took a step back like I didn't want any of it rubbing off on me. Niko was one of those people you never imagine taking off their clothes. Even in the shower, there had to be some layer of him that wouldn't fully surrender, some last moment of personality that would never give way. And of course I wondered, who wouldn't really, what his friends might look like. Are there ghettos of beauty and ugliness, each with its genetic border guards? Do beautiful people truck with others of the same kind so they can feel ordinary? My Sudbury comrades and new neighbours, even the people I saw on the subway, all belonged to the middle class: neither beautiful nor ugly, we were the ones who watched. Only this didn't sound like watching.

We stepped outside through an insect screen gaffer-taped to the remains of a window. It wasn't a spot anyone but Niko would have called a deck, just a flattened stretch of shingles that provided an occasional perch. But he was wondering if tonight it might possibly serve those guests who wanted to air out.

'It looks pretty shaky up here, Niko. One good breeze and someone's overboard.'

'Do you really think so? Having to come to the rescue would be the height of fantastic. Hand-over-handing them back from the edge ... Imagine.'

'Who said anything about rescue?'

I don't know what he was like before he moved here, but there was something unspeakable that he dared me to share with him. Niko had developed an appetite for awkwardness, he grew large on it the way others ballooned on Ho-Hos or cheese blintzes. He was a magnet for whatever was young and untried, and while no one could accuse him of being a predator exactly, not in the usual sense anyway, it was generally understood that he loved watching people fail. The younger and more beautiful the better. He had once spent a long evening crawling through the Scarborough mud with a fifteen-year-old hitchhiker, looking for his car keys, which he claimed to have thrown away, along with the remains of an E-Z Boy burger and a fistful of cold fries. 'It was *glorious*, Auden, the look on the boy's face, like he was never ever going to get home. And just when it seemed we would have to give up and spend the night in the car, there they were, the keys, like *God* had pointed them out to us.'

We stepped back into his living room and I felt the warm light spot the back of my neck and burn a quarter-sized hole that my hearing leaked through. The window announced cars rounding the winner's circle in a warm blur while streetlights raged through colours one after another, as if they couldn't decide. I sunk down into the couch while Niko busied himself in the kitchen filling ice-cube trays. Quiet. I had never heard quiet run so deep. He stepped back into the living room and I could see his lips moving without a sound. I held a glass up to my cheek and watched him throw his hands up in the air and laugh. I might have laughed too. I put my drink down on the floor, but it was so soft it just swallowed up the glass. Niko was still laughing and pushed me back so that I was lying on the couch facing the quiet ceiling. I might have lain there a long time, it was hard to tell.

One of Niko's charges held the door open when I arrived, a great, moon-faced smile of a girl who said, 'Glad you could make it,' as if she really meant it. She looked maybe eighteen going on twelve, symmetrical pigtails bouncing as she walked me through Niko's postage-stamp kitchen, where we stopped long enough for me to put a beer in each fist. Nothing worse than having to stand around wondering what to do with your hands at an orgy, right? She led me into the back, and it occurred to me that this was the only other room in Niko's apartment. Privacy was definitely on the shelf for the evening.

There were about a dozen people circling the floor, and every one of them on the sunny side of twenty, young and poreless and beaming back at me with names like Brix and Svet and Lou, which I forgot as soon as it left their Pepsodent glows. Niko was in the corner chatting up a heavy-metal blond who was so thin I could have laid a thatch of straw on his head and swept the room with him. What was I doing here?

'Auden, glad you could drop by. Stan, this is Auden.'

'Hi.'

'Hi.'

'Stan's thinking of getting a facial tattoo, aren't you, Stan?'

Stan looked at Niko and then over at me, weary over the long march of his eighteen years. He'd already come back from the end of the world, that's what his eyes were telling me, though his scrub was a little too fresh for life on the streets. I wondered if he wasn't still living at home with Mom and Dad, the acne support system of his face wrapped in hip-hop cans and net-speak. The kid looked like borrowed rhymes, like he had downloaded a personality especially for tonight. So what made me so nervous?

'There's a bar code, like they use in the SuperSave and shit. For like shit they don't, you know, have a thing for. A category. And these things like they could be anything, right? Like strawberries and fucking cream or like whatever. But all this shit that doesn't belong has like this bar code on it that just means whatever. That's what I want to get, right?'

'You want to get a bar code inked on your face?' I asked him, not quite sure I was catching the rap.

'I'm gonna, like, wear it. Loud and proud.' He smiled at me and I found myself smiling back, wishing my needs could be laid up where everyone could see them.

I swung both beers in the general direction of my face, trying to wash down the bad feelings. We were here, weren't we? Weren't we here? Because this was an o-r-g-y, I tried not to look at anyone too long, which mostly meant I made detailed studies of the ashtray and the way the long tongues of wood didn't quite meet to form the floor. Everyone was a little tight, like we were all in the green room waiting for the show to start. Niko was loving this, for him this was going to be the best part. The waiting and fugitive glances, the shy smiles that might mean yes, maybe later, okay if you like. Or not now, I need another drink, and then, surely then.

There was a couple on the couch, paler-than-pale brunettes, sunless lip-lockers who fumbled with tops not entirely relieved of duty. I tried not to stare, and caught them in glimpses out of the corner of my eye, when a tidy Szechuan girl rubbed them each across their shoulders and offered up a joint. They looked over in surprise and she tendered them a shy smile and pushed on, headed in my direction. There was something easy in the way she did it, no need for headlights here, never going to hit anything on these roads. Nothing but green country. Our country.

'You must be Niko's friend.' She offered me the bomb and I took it, just to be polite. Weed was something I usually did to take the edge off and right now I needed all the edge I could get. I gave it a long haul.

'And you?' I gasped through the smoke.

'I know Dee,' she said, still smiling, nodding over to the girl on the couch.

'Is that her boyfriend?'

'I guess you could call him that,' she said through eyes that narrowed just enough to see if I was kidding. 'For tonight, I mean. I don't know. His name's Ben.'

'I'm Auden.'

'I know, you're Niko's friend. I thought Niko didn't have any friends, except for Steve, of course, but Steve doesn't really have any friends either, so it figures. You know?' Her words erupted from that soft face like a warm blog widget spitting headlines.

'Who is Steve?' I asked, trying to ignore her friend on the couch. Dee, was it? She was naked now, grinding herself down on her one-night boyfriend who was steadily losing his grip on the couch universe. There were a couple of others huddled in the corners, necking mostly, but for now Dee was the main attraction. Everyone did their best not to stare.

'You don't know Steve Reinke?' she asked, still holding the bomb. 'He's really the one who started all this.' She waved her hand distractedly around the room. 'Although it's funny, when you see him, the last thing on your mind is sex. You know what I mean?'

I finished the first beer and was looking for a place to put it when she calmly relieved my grip and stashed it in a corner generously furnished with forgotten receipts and never-used sporting equipment. Did I know what she meant?

'Everybody here – ' she said as she paused to wrinkle her nose at a slack-faced skateboard refugee who already looked a little unwound '– well, almost everyone here – took the same English class, right? And then some bad Asian flu took out the teacher, the substitute and half the class, so they were trying to find someone to come in. Monday morning, and who should walk through the door but Steve. I don't think Steve ever gets sick, he doesn't have enough of a body for sick to hold on to. You know what I mean?'

'Meee-ow,' I laughed, raking my nails through the air. The beer had settled in nicely.

'Sorry. So, anyway, instead of walking us through the rest of Shakespeare's *Merchant of Venus*, he said he had something to show us. A videotape. Something he'd made himself.'

'Weird.'

'Steve is weird. So he shows us this tape, right? And it's really fucking long, excuse my French. It's about an hour or something, and at first it seems like nothing's going on, it's just, you know, signal noise before the show starts, and then we realize that this is the show. Although by then, okay, a lot of people had nodded off or asked to be excused or something. To tell you the truth, I didn't catch any of that until later because, for the first time, like maybe the first time ever, I was paying attention, or finally had some idea of what attention really was. You know? And all the time he's talking – on the videotape, I mean – Steve never stops talking, and it's funny, because I can't remember anything he said. Nothing at all. And when I asked Dee about it later, she couldn't remember either. You know what I mean?'

'I know what you mean,' I told her, not understanding a word, but hoping she wouldn't stop either.

'So maybe a bunch of people had already left, and maybe I got bored with being bored, but I started making out this body in the middle of all that static and noise, and not just one body but all kinds of people were up in there and the crazy thing was that they were talking to each other without making a sound. They were all, you know, making sense to each other just by ... '

'What?'

'Touching. They were just touching each other, and that was enough.'

'Like Dee, you mean?' I asked her, hoping she wouldn't look over to where her friend lay helpless in the grip of some new communication paradigm. I felt that if she stopped looking at me, even for a moment, I was going to fall over, and even though I'd arrived too late to read the fine print, I knew that was definitely not orgy protocol. Mercifully, she held my eyes steady while I finished off the bomb and she started up another.

'When school was out, Steve let us pinch the video for homework, but now we don't need the tape anymore.'

'Yeah,' I mumbled, trying to hold on. The spliff was really taking hold, lifting me into gravity-optional sightlines. Stranger still, whenever she talked it felt as if I were saying the words, only they were coming out of her mouth. Why wasn't she handing me back the bomb?

'Most classrooms are machines for producing language. Even math is a conversation between numbers, right? But what if talking wasn't a question of mouth-to-mouth? What if your whole body could talk?' She paused, and I felt the wooden floors take a long breath so they could keep holding us up. All that effort and who ever noticed?

'That's why we come here,' she concluded, and I followed her look back over to her nappy-haired comrade who had finally struggled out of his too-tight clothing. He was busy rubbing himself across Dee's flanks as if he were making a gravestone relief.

'You mean the way she's, that they're both ... ' I stammered.

'They're studying together. Yes. I can show you if you like.'

'I don't know, I think, it's not that you're not lovely and all, but ... '

'Next time.'

'Sure, next time,' I said, wondering if I'd ever set foot in here again. So this was Steve's idea. Steve Reinke. Funny, Niko had never mentioned him. But then Niko was always soft on names. When I said I didn't know him, some mix of wonder and curiosity settled over that round face, like I'd told her I'd never heard of the pope. Steve fucking Reinke. Who was this guy anyway?

Niko regained the living room wearing something that bore a striking resemblance to a bathrobe. 'You're right, Niko,' I wanted to tell him, 'terry cloth is much sexier than leather.' Only a helpless stutter came out of my mouth instead. He put his arm around me and bussed me on the cheek and whispered under his breath, 'Relax, Auden, they *like* you.' I knew then that it was working, the long hours I'd spent rubbing away the person I used to be were finally coming due. And then I excused myself to go to the bathroom and threw up.

God made the world in seven days, but you never hear about the mornings. Mornings must have been hard even then. The beginning of my days were filled with inventory and roll call, making sure everything was still there. White tongue and swollen feet were reliable companions, along with bulging lymph nodes and muscles lathered with a deep night sweat, as if the real work of the body were being done while sleeping. I would strip the drenched sheets off the foam block, wondering at the smell. Was that me? Of course there was the fear I wouldn't be getting up at all, that I'd wake up on the other side, a shade forced to watch while professionals took away my body before it could spread its awful secret. I was the symptom of this illness. My personality, the words I used, my likes and dislikes, were simply its effects.

But there was one thought that never failed to comfort me, tucking me away each night with a supersized grin planted across the remains of my face. No matter how imperfect my condition, I could rely on the fact that most would never notice, being far too busy with their own versions of heaven and hell. Whether cramming for Johnson, or riding the transit home, I was passing, and in this oblivion of indifference I left my illness behind, if only for a moment. I was well again, or at least as well as the worried faces that surrounded me. Of course I was dying, but who had time to notice? And the more I started looking like the people on television, where problems large and small were disarmed with catchy one-liners and a toss of designer hair, the better everyone felt. I'd be six feet of lies if I didn't admit it made me feel a little better too. Sure, I was just going through the motions, but I was learning to like the motions. They suited me, or at least the new person I was becoming.

On the subway I watched a young boy tag his mother who had fallen asleep. He scrawled his marker over her arms and face and what looked like it might have been an expensive handbag. When their stop came, he stole away and left her there to snooze. I guessed remorse had come to him after all, a little late to make any difference. When my stop came, she was still fast asleep, with the touch of her boy covering her like a second skin. I left without a word, grateful and ashamed for the distraction of someone else's botheration. At least the illness that time-shared my body, the intruder that had become my new home, was temporarily invisible. I stopped in at the variety store looking for magazine distractions but gave up and chatted up the owner, a towering man in a suit that might have fit him as a child, with a single lock of hair crossing his shaved scalp. Whenever he turned the other cheek I could see the words *Love Me* inked across his cheekbone. Too bad it was invisible for the one who needed it most.

'Whatever remains of people is what media can store and communicate.' Niko said it was a quote from Kittler, some German pooh-bah with a brain so large they needed to build a special room for him to lecture in. Whatever. Niko had been out, as in out of town, though he didn't let on where exactly. And he was in a bit of a mood this morning, which was rare. Mostly Niko didn't have moods, he was as reliable as the Duracell Bunny. Or was that the Easter Bunny?

'You might have stayed longer, Auden.'

'At the orgy?'

'Aren't we acting a little royal?'

'We? I thought I was doing all the acting,' I told him, reclining on a couch that would never look quite the same after watching young love appear so much like work. Not that there was anywhere else to plant. Niko was wearing one of his funny hats, something the Whos from Whoville might look comfortable in, so it was hard to take anything he said all that seriously. What surprised me was that no matter what we talked about, I found it hard to take myself all that seriously either.

'I felt like an old man, Niko. And by the time I sit down and talk out my illness ... '

'No one's asking you to explain anything, Auden. They're hardly twenty, they don't believe in explanations.'

'Well, it's not exactly hard-on material, is it?'

'I thought you might take it in the wrong direction. Really, it's the only reason I didn't invite you sooner.'

I watched him pace off the tiles of his apartment in a slow-motion hopscotch. He was trying to tell me something, but he couldn't just come out and say it.

'Hey, what is it?'

'What?' Niko replied, his voice a thousand miles away.

'What is it?' I insisted.

'What is what?'

'You're in a mood.'

'I don't have moods, Auden. I'm as regular as the Duracell Bunny. Or is that the Easter Bunny?'

'So why do you sound like you're about to jump out of your sneakers?'

He gave me a look that was Niko's shorthand for *I'm having large thoughts and I need to be alone now so they can spread across the flat.* I searched for the dark windbreaker I'd tossed at the front door and took the stairs two at a time until I was back on the street. The sky looked anxious, and little wonder. All the faces from the retirement home had wound up on the bodies of kids while kids' faces were propped up inside suit jackets and commuter glances. It was time to go back to the gym.

I wasn't big on hospitals. Even lingering in the vicinity seemed reckless. The worry was always the same: no matter what the pretext was going in, they might never let you leave. But when I got word that my old high school friend-of-a-friend Jorge was slipping away in North York General, there was no way around it.

Not wanting to run into any of the old gang, or any of the new gang, for that matter, I booked off early with Johnson, who gave me a long look that asked, *Why did you bother coming in at all if you're only going to work six hours?* Never mind the two-hour conference call I transcribed right through what most liked to call lunchtime. But I wanted to go see Jorge without a crowd scene, and while I had some sense of his sprawling best-friend directory, I figured the afternoon would be pretty quiet.

When I got up to the tenth floor, the nurse didn't need to look up Jorge in the computer. 'Room 1027,' she announced brightly, staring up into my face as if she were searching for something she'd lost. 'Straight down the hall and take a right.' I stood at his door for a moment, long enough to hear the stage-whispered conspiracies of soap-opera stars on those extra-small TV sets they must make just for hospitals and a choked whimper of response from the bed, followed by deeply regular breathing. When I stepped inside, the tears were still fresh on his cheek and he'd fallen fast asleep. Possibly in the same breath.

He looked about ten kilos lighter than the last time I'd seen him, and the IVs and monitors weren't doing him any favours. 'Hey, Jorge,' I stage-whispered, and when he didn't stir I wanted to lam it out of there, but the wrath of Johnson made me inch closer to the bedside.

'Hey, Jorge,' I said again, nudging him ever so gently until he shot bolt upright and shouted, 'What the fuck do you want?'

I could tell by the look in his eyes he didn't know where he was, but then he pulled me into focus and broke into a big hometown smile and we kind of hugged. He couldn't really get all the way around because of the tubing, and as he drew close I could feel every bone underneath the sad hospital slip.

'What are you doing down here?' he asked me.

'Same as you, came for the free beds and the good food.'

'They got you booked in too, Auden?' he asked, suddenly serious.

'No, no, I'm good. And those gowns do nothing for my figure. You look great, though, Jorge,' I assured him, shining it up a little bit, but I don't think he caught the lie. Instead I could see Sudbury coming back up on his register, maybe some beer lark, a stolen car or two, a bonfire out at the pit. Back when he could lay claim to a body that wasn't busy dying, even though the city around us was.

'You ever see JD or Sal or Matt?' he asked.

'No, no, I only see you.'

'You softhead.'

'I can't help it. I come here to the big city and have to play dumb, otherwise it makes all the Toronto wheels feel uncomfortable. We can't let on we know everything, right? We're small-town boys. We have to *yes sir, no sir*, until it's our turn, isn't that the plan?'

'So when is it going to be our turn?'

'Tomorrow, babe, it's always our turn tomorrow.'

'Right,' he nodded to me, suddenly tired again.

I pulled up one of those folding auditorium chairs and he held out his hand and I took it and he gave me a squeeze and smiled and I squeezed him right back. All I wanted to do was run and go to bed and not get back out of it for a week or until the memory of all this was far far away, but I sat there and smiled right back at him.

'Don't go yet, okay?' he asked, so worn all of a sudden that he could hardly keep his eyes open.

'I'm right here, Jorge.'

It was like someone had scooped out the person I knew and left this behind. I felt that if I squeezed too hard his hand would shatter in a hundred directions. Jorge's breathing became regular and I looked past the green monitors and tubes and Kleenex box and saw a note scribbled on the backside of a hospital bib.

> Before leaving my friends behind, I became convinced that they would be no use to me where I was going. That's what I told myself when I couldn't face them, when anyone, anyone at all, was too much. And I wasn't much use to them, was I? With my constant fevers and sudden pains. 'No, I really want to stay home tonight, you just go out and have a good time, okay?' Is that when I started hating them? Is that when Philip and Norrie and Abigail became Them? Part of the army of normals. The healthy. I mentioned none of this, of course, to anyone. My secret was a grave designed for single occupancy. I was teaching myself how to die one unanswered phone call at a time.

His hand had gone limp and I folded it back onto his chest. I got up out of the chair like a cat-and-dog burglar and stole backwards out of the room, sending him the silent promise that I would come back soon, but knowing I probably wouldn't. It wasn't until I was out in the hallway that I realized my face was wet. I wiped it with the end of my sleeve and started back down the long hall, trying not to look into any of the passing rooms. A gurney passed loaded up with temporary hope. I strode confidently towards the elevators and then jogged into the stairwell at the last moment, pausing to collect myself at the ground floor before taking the revolving door outside. No one looked back, no one got hurt.

When I ran by Niko's apartment after work he wasn't around, even though he was always around at that hour. The mailbox brimmed with flyers. Next day, same playlist. Confident that he would never hear them, I began leaving answering-machine messages that used only words that clung like perfume and that would induce even the most indifferent listener to follow my every command. Though perhaps Niko's incommunicado was his way of saying he needed a little space.

One evening after I'd had a particularly uneventful day at work, Niko called from the airport. He was panting hard, as if he were dialling direct from the finish line. He said he was on his way to London on a one-way ticket. London, England? There was something missing in his voice, the little murmur that ran underneath his speaking that always asked, *What's in it for me?* He didn't sound himself without it.

'It's my father. He's not well.'

'I'm sorry to hear that, Niko. You don't sound so handsome yourself.'

'He can't stop coughing, he's lost a lot of weight and there's these marks on him.'

'Your father?'

'I said my fucking father, didn't I?'

AIDS. The word Niko and I never mentioned because I wouldn't let him. The first time it came out of his mouth it sounded so wrong, and I'd had enough of wrong in my life. When I told Niko about my diagnosis he didn't seem surprised, just rolled it around in his mouth for a while before deciding that yes, it would have to do. Indifference had never tasted so sweet. But I could hardly believe the word on Niko's father. The account-ant for Grimsby and Shires, the tidy man in the hand-cut suit who arrived, Niko wearily announced, exactly once a year, and took Niko to the same overpriced steak house near the market for the same dinner sans vegetables. Vegetables, so far as Niko's father was concerned, were for losers. Eat a broccoli spear and you might as well book yourself right into the seniors' home. Who was going to tell the bad joke about the elephant and the bartender, or bend a fork prong to use as a toothpick or simply be The Thing That Never Changes? Against the shipwreck of Niko's apartment, the orgies he hosted as a not-so-innocent bystander, the going-nowhere jobs, his father was the last part of forever he still had a grip on. And now the old man had AIDS? I couldn't put it together.

'I'm so sorry, Niko. I don't what to say.'

'I know, I didn't call. I haven't really told anyone because ... '

'I know.'

'I know you know.'

'Yeah.'

'Yeah, well.' Niko sounded tight enough to launch into temporary orbit, his voice high-pitched and sticky with tension, though it could have been just a bad run of wires from the airport.

'It was Steve, Steve Reinke, who actually told me about it.'

'Steve Reinke?' I asked, trying to keep the disbelief out of my voice.

'Steve called me and said there's something wrong with my father and that I should go see him right away.'

'Steve Reinke knows your father?' I asked him again.

'My father knows Steve.'

'Oh.'

'A lot of people know Steve.'

'He sure gets around. So you talked to your father?'

'We talked.'

'And he really said … '

'He was pretty surprised.'

'I'll bet.'

'He didn't know how I'd found out.'

'I'll bet he was surprised.'

'He asked if I would come and see him, and he's never asked before, not for anything really.'

'I'm sorry, Niko.'

'That's my flight. I've got to go now. Take care, okay?'

'Take care yourself,' I hollered into the dead line but he was gone, already swallowed by disaster. It was the last time we ever spoke, and I started missing him before I'd hung up the receiver.

It was never difficult to tell when happiness wasn't leaning towards Johnson. One of the perks of the rich is that their bad moods are designed as shareware. *If I can't sleep properly, I'm going to have to remortgage your house, cancel your credit or, at least, no morning coffee in the office.*

'Yes, sir?'

'I need the Henderson file snap snap, and these,' Johnson fairly shouted, gesturing to a metre-deep avalanche of paper, 'need to be summarized and refiled before you leave today.'

'Yes,' I said, hoping the balance of his favourite word would calm him.

'Yes, yes,' he exclaimed and jumped across the floor. As his mood darkened, Johnson would increasingly resemble animal life from his native Australia, alternately slithering or hopping. No one dared to mention it to him, of course. Let the other high-flying execs deal with the marsupials.

I began tucking into the day's first unreasonable request when I felt the room warming. I lurched towards the open window only to be caught short by Johnson's kangaroo act.

'Where do you think you're going?' he asked, but I could only mumble in reply. All the heat in the office seemed to be coming from Johnson himself, standing in front of him was like facing a blast furnace. It wasn't long before his face grew whiter than a toothpaste ad and I felt myself falling, slowly falling, into the infinitely soft carpet. Why had I never noticed this beautiful carpet before? Brown shag pile, each renewable bamboo fibre like a pillow.

Johnson accepted food poisoning as a plausible cause and I was sent home for a few days. The temp agency had a replacement at my desk in under an hour, and this arrangement soon became a workday staple. I worked as much as I could, and left the rest for Cary, an almost-teenager and peerless filer who worshipped Johnson with predictable results: everything was always Cary's fault and new problems were constantly arising on his watch that I would be called upon to straighten out. Johnson sang my praises until even I was tired of hearing them, but sure enough, Cary quickly became indispensable, and came to count on my regular bouts of 'work-induced fatigue.' Johnson began calling us the 'alternating current.'

Even the most fatal illnesses have weekends. Not Saturday and Sunday weekends, but pauses, respites, chinooks of health that might blow in suddenly and unexpectedly. There were days when Johnson couldn't tell and I couldn't tell either. I regaled him with tales of imagined sexual adventures that he relished almost as much as I enjoyed telling them. He particularly enjoyed group encounters, risky public situations and humiliations of any kind. I was sure to include liberal amounts of each in my recountings. Back home, I listened to reports from Paris and New York that labs were working around the clock to find a magic bullet against AIDS, though they were not armed with any sense of calamity. Instead, their urgency stemmed from good old-fashioned greed. It was clear by now that whoever cracked this nut would have their name storied by unborn schoolchildren. Nobels were already warming with the best labs money could buy. The race was on. And we were grateful for that, because we knew greed, had dipped our own fingers in it. It was trustworthy and reliable. If anything would save us, it would be greed.

I tried to picture them, unyielding men and women already looking old in their white coats, checking the numbers, then checking them again. This had become a math war. Already, endless stat columns were marshalled around the certainty of my death. Our deaths. Most of us figured these efforts weren't exactly on our side because we'd already tripped a little too far from science. The numbers were running for the ones not yet infected, the millions who couldn't see us. Or saw us and didn't care. Or saw us and said, Not me. Never, not me. My neighbours, sure, every apartment in the apartment building, my whole goddamn family, but not me.

And then there was Steve. Steve Reinke. His name sounded like a badly crumpled fender. 'Nice car, too bad about the Reinke, don't know if we'll be able to hammer that out.' I don't know why, but I had somehow attached to him the most dangerous of feelings, the ones I had tried to keep at arm's length ever since I'd got word from the underaged doctor in the clinic. Hope. I was starting to hope again that there might be a way through this after all, that there could be life after death or, at least, after diagnosis.

I tried not to blame him for it, the one I'd never met, the Steve that had lain inside Niko's talk, glittering like fool's gold. Hope is also a four-letter word. It seemed I'd lived without it for so long, content to practice a democracy of feeling: I love my chair, I love my breakfast, I love you. Papa doesn't play favourites, not with his emotions.

I had a friend who had a tattoo scorched across his ass that read *Abandon Hope All Ye Who Enter*. When he found out he was positive, it was as if he'd known all along. He couldn't abide anyone dropping a mention of his tat, his beautiful secret of a scar let out where everyone could see it. I heard he locked himself up in his apartment and stayed there until his time came. He'd kill me for saying so if he wasn't already dead.

It was JD who tracked me down and left word about Jorge. JD was the kind of pretty that even straight men turned to look at as he came through the door. He left Sudbury on his own steam, heading south to catch a Britpop sensation and winding up on a bedroom tour with the bass guitarist. When the last auditorium folded its seats, he was already tending bar at some former rock palace and had invited me how many times, but even on weekends when I had nothing to do but count sidewalk cracks I couldn't seem to find the way.

'Jorge didn't make it last night,' JD told me.

No one pronounced *dead* anymore because too many were dead. No one said, 'He begged a God he never believed in for one more day and cursed all his friends and cried until he was dry and screamed for life and then he was gone.' Because it could happen anytime, anywhere. There was a tacit agreement among us, the ones who had been left behind, the survivors, that we would say, 'He didn't make it last night.' Because we were still making it, climbing the mountain, even as others around us fell back. And while it was obvious to one and all that there was hardly enough left of them to die, we consoled ourselves with the fiction that they didn't want to go on. They were not unable but unwilling to draw up and start another day.

'I saw him maybe a week ago now, it's hard to remember,' I said.

'Yes, me too,' JD told me and all of a sudden the phone felt cold and far away and I wanted to gather up my old friend and hold him. But because my mouth was filled with wanting Jorge to get through and make it and because I hadn't even allowed myself to say the words, I didn't have any now. A neighbour's daughter shrieked nearby in pain or pleasure. Footsteps in the hall and then a moment of quiet before more followed. And then the terrible silence of surrender. I thanked JD for calling.

Jorge's funeral had a homespun air, some dime-store show business clung to it that managed warm and awkward in equal, heartbreaking measures that reminded us all of the way Jorge used to be, before the illness got hold of him. While still in Sudbury, he had come across the story of Charles V, some Spanish pugilist who had devoted the last few years of his life to the rehearsal of his own funeral, which he attended as a spectator, solemnly looking on as mourners wept and censers swayed. What an idea! Rehearsals! Jorge threw himself into it with a grim exuberance, managing just two in the end, gaudy extravaganzas filled with Chippendale strippers, poets and performance artists. Jorge himself delivered a final oration from the casket, a karaoke version of, what else, 'Sisters Are Doin' It for Themselves.'

I have to admit I was initially repulsed, telling him, 'Jorge, I don't know. I think you're really asking for it.' To which he replied, 'I don't need to ask, Auden, I already have it.' But he made it look like fun somehow, and while we felt we'd touched everything that concerned death and its science of small indignities and slow declines, Jorge had shown us another side after all. It really was possible to die with a smile on your face and Aretha on your lips.

Now the rehearsals were over, and we were gathered for a last time in the funeral home, clapping our hands to Andy, another Sudbury refugee, who was shaking out one of his trademark two-word poems. Andy was so shy he pretended not to recognize anyone, not even his mother, who followed him everywhere. His determined stutter gave his reading of 'MORE. LIGHT. MORE. LIGHT' a nearly unbearable poignancy. JD found me in the scrum and we hugged at last, and I felt something soft for a moment behind all those years at the gym. His perfect, overly long lashes were wet and I tried not to look at him in the same way that every other man in the room looked at him, this airbrushed chauffeur of catastrophe.

Sexually speaking, JD had never met a man he didn't like. It was as if he had to make up for his natural gifts by giving them away to whoever asked. 'It's like a smorgasbord, Auden,' he told me once. 'You don't pig out on one item, you try a little of everything.' He was the first person I knew who was infected. The first to make the long drive south to Toronto. Miraculously, he had outlasted us all, and always looked terrific. I tried not to hate him for it.

'That's him,' said JD, nodding towards a man in the next row.

'What?' I asked him.

'That's him, the guy you're looking for. Steve, right?'

'That's Steve Reinke?'

'I'm telling you.'

Steve had weak features, a nose that wasn't entirely sure, eyes that were so milky blue they were nearly out of focus and a chin that slumped back into his neck. It was a face without bones or definition, the better to serve as a mirror for his surroundings. I walked slowly towards him, excusing myself, feeling the crowd part reluctantly until I could smell the aftershave off him, a clement version of those paper evergreens that hung from rear-view mirrors. I was instantly taken back, lost in the feeling and, for just a breath, happier than I'd been in months.

His alert, overly large head made a jog to the left, and then craned over to the right. Even with all that death in the room he could feel someone looking at him, and while I took in the search, I couldn't pull my eyes off him. Some customary force field of shame and dignity had temporarily vacationed, and the hunch of his observation nagged until at last he turned to face me and I looked straight back. It was like watching TV, I thought, and then very slowly the TV broke into a wide smile and I felt the room drain of colour, suspended in a whitening fever. I can't remember anything like the commotion of the fall, surely it was nothing that dramatic, I might have wobbled in my joints for a moment, might have even reached towards a neighbour's steadying hand until gravity reasserted itself. A stranger's broad smile revealed rows of uneven teeth and a cloud of mint. I could feel my knees and elbows pooling as I excused myself and made my way to the very back, past the rows of fine suits that had suddenly grown too large for their occupants. It was as if we'd all lockstepped into the same dream of a body larger than ourselves and bought the same clothes to grow into. As I shuffled towards the chair sanctuaries at the back of the room, there was more than one pair of hands reaching to touch an arm or shoulder or the back of my neck with unspoken reassurance. With every step they grew smaller, and I was growing smaller too, until the chairs in front of me looked like they had been made for some future race of giants. I reached up for a cushion grown impossibly far away, and borne with the memory of Steve's smile, I threw myself towards it and a new beginning.

Dr. Phil is a large professional man with a voice like children whispering in the dark. He was a regular on Oprah so I saw him pretty often. There were some weeks, when the guests were threatening to crack under the weight of parental neglect, erectile dysfunction or high school bullying, that I might have seen him every day. Much more than my friends, at any rate.

Dr. Phil said that while you might meet hundreds of people in your life, there are no more than half a dozen on the A-list. If your life were a movie, these names would appear before the title.

There's something else he said that quickened my pulse. Dr. Phil insisted that accompanying the six (more or less) guest stars, there were just eight significant events. The first was birth. Don't ask me how he knew, but when I looked into that kind, smiling face, I understood it must be true. The eyes of Dr. Phil had seen the end of our days and come back to tell the story, and not only was I grateful to him, I'd started counting. Eight moments. That's how long it took to get to the raw, beating heart of a life.

He was sitting right beside me when I came to on one of the overstuffed chairs that sealed the back of the funeral home. Once a parlour, twice a home. Steve smiled and asked me a question I didn't understand at first. I had to let my ears rerun through the overly loud orations until I realized he was asking, *What took you so long?* His eyes never leaving mine. And I was startled, because here was the voice that belonged inside my head. Not the voice that made to-do lists or punished me even when things seemed fly, but the one that accompanied my reading.

In the alternating current of my work life, Cary was busy worshipping at his Johnson sanctum while I lay in bed reading. Turning the page. Books promised escape and the solace of a soothing, accompanying voice that read the book inside me, silently healing. Now this same voice had leapt into the mouth of this stranger, Steve. Steve Reinke. While Jorge's funeral swirled around us, Steve told me that I had to write a book of my own, and that we would meet in the coming months so that he could tell it to me. It would narrate the story of his life, which was not a story at all, as it turned out, but a kind of operating manual for a machine that he had spent his life perfecting, and that one day would appear in the world looking to the innocent observer just like a book.

I didn't embrace his Steveness right away. I couldn't run into his arms or call him right over and whisper the secrets I didn't yet know I had. For one thing, I didn't understand how he had managed to get his voice, that satisfyingly mellifluous drawl, up into my head. Or had I jumped the voice that was in my head into his?

Around the corner from the apartment, there was a bar that never bothered posting a name, a converted magazine shop with a worn set of numbers across the face and a door that was always busy closing. Some people called it the Thing, everybody else just called it the place on the corner. I knew that drinking wasn't the first-choice accompaniment to bedrest and barbell squats and, worse, it belonged to my former life, the one I had worked so diligently to leave behind. But the signless sign offered promises each day I managed to leave the apartment. A little convenience went such a long way.

I didn't recognize Steve at first. He was a slouch of polyester holding up one end of the bar, that's all. I settled in across from the tender and took a pull from a local stout. Later, when I asked Steve if he was bothered by the fact that I failed to recognize him, he looked surprised. 'But I didn't want to be noticed,' he told me, as if it had been up to him. And maybe it was. So when I looked over the bar's polish, it was a perfect stranger I saw raising his mug to meet my own. Our glasses exactly alike, golden twins sharing a secret.

For every brew there is a new kind of mug, each competing with the others in the brewer's eternal quest for the perfect drink. In order to make their wares more closely resemble desire itself, the brewmeisters here had cast the mouths of their most dedicated patrons in glass. After years of careful experimentation, they unveiled their new creation: the Adam of bar glasses! The usual mug had been cut away at the lip, opened in a cascade of glass that lifted up into the drinker's mouth where it swam across the face. The neighbourhood emptied as revellers herded into the bar, and tourists soon began planning trips around the landmark discovery. Business grew brisk, if solitary, the experience of the brew so complete that even the highest forms of conversation seemed banal. All too soon, the pub grew silent and emptied as its patrons returned to the imperfect comfort of their former haunts, raising ordinary glasses of indifferent brew, finding in their escape from perfection the possibility of happiness.

We used the old mug as an ashtray, though it still made me uncomfortable somehow, staring back at us with the accusation of once-utopias. We were all born young.

'Do you ... ?' I paused, looking for the word, except there wasn't one now.

'Fuck?' He smiled helpfully, soft eyes melting in the overheads. How many times had he been asked like this by a stranger in a bar longing for escape in someone else's fantasy? But I knew it was all right, I could tell by the smooth landing pad of his face that he had come for the same reason. To leave himself behind, to give himself over to the meat and its presentation. Here at the bar, and afterwards, in the other place, at his place or mine, we were only bodies. The relief this brought was better than orgasm, better than touching even. To become a body.

I still didn't recognize him at all. His skin was a kind of camouflage, allowing him to meet the same person over and over, enjoy the same conversation and, best of all, recount the same jokes.

'A blind man and his guide dog walk into a bar. As soon as he gets inside the door, he picks up the dog and swings it over his head. When the bartender asks him what he's doing, the blind man answers, "Just looking around."'

I didn't move in the chair as he ran a hand over my shoulders and down my back to the small pinched nerves at the base. He never looked at me. He stared, as if distracted, into a remote corner of the room, though this didn't upset me. Not at all. Only I couldn't stop my face from asking, never tiring of the question, *Who will love me?*

Steve walked me to the back of the club, where it was so dark I couldn't see my hands in front of me. Was he still there? We kissed slowly and for a long time, praying together. I could feel the shaking start, my lips caving at the feeling, it had been so long since this body, my body, deserved anything like this. I know it wasn't the right word but it was the one that rose up to meet him, *deserved*, deserved anything at all but needles and tests and pills, and now there was someone refusing all that.

His hands, when they touched, were so soft, like question marks running down my back. 'Like this?' they asked. 'Like this?' And I tried to stuff *grateful*, and *thank you* and *please yes* and *I love you* back into the soft hole and feel it, really feel it. I tried to jack out of my head for a minute and let the searching hands fill me until I could begin to let go. Small tears ran down my face, grateful for the darkness, but I was still soft. Too many hands in those plastic E-Z Wipe gloves had smeared and poked and run their professional fingers over these same parts asking, 'Here? Does it hurt here?' His hands – the machines of pleasure, the machines of science – were turning in the same cycle, which didn't quite, not quite, take me there. I fell limp with a weak smile and pulled him towards me and held him, just held him there unmoving.

When it was over, to my complete surprise, he asked if I'd like to stop by tomorrow if I wasn't too busy. I was already in the wind, circulating in free-form patterns of small weather. Ready. The next day we learned to talk. To say the words after *I want*. We became friends.

The phone call I was dreading didn't begin well. I had rehearsed it so many times, with every variation of response plotted on a chart with different-coloured markers, that by the time I hit the speed dial I was numb for opening night. I'd over-rehearsed.

'No, Johnson, I'm not taking a vacation. I've had some medical complications ... '

How my sometimes boss hated listening to the word *no*. It was always preferable to say yes, even if I was saying no. It would have been simpler to bend him over my knee and redden his cheeks.

'Look, Auden, we're trying to run a little insurance firm here, and I've been relying on that inexpert colleague of yours ... '

'Cary.'

'Yes, Cary. And despite the fact that he seems to do nothing but run from one end of the office to the other all day, he just can't keep up.'

'Cary's a very dedicated player, sir. I really think he's found his calling under your kind ... ' And then I laid down a coughing fit because I couldn't come up with the rest.

We were off the game card. I had started with the fat green marker, bent into yellow and had now strayed past the margins. I didn't know where we were headed, and for a moment I didn't care whether I lost my job or not. I would go back to the temp agency when I could stay awake long enough to ride the streetcar there.

'I want you to come in tomorrow, Auden.'

'Tomorrow?'

'Yes, I've got meetings with Williams and Hendrix and I'm going to need both of you around. I know I can count on you.'

I had a feeling that he wasn't ready to trust young Cary with his escort bookings just yet, and that I would be asked to make arrangements for the upcoming weeks. It would buy me some string, so I climbed into bed early, hoping that a twelve-hour bed shift would be enough to get me out the door. That night I had my first dream about Steve. He had four scars on his face, long and complicated scars that covered his eyes, nose and mouth. He was sent to the nation's capital where his face became a cherished object of prophecy that state seers used to determine policy. The rest of his body was encased in something very much like a coffin, and remained unseen. They were never interested in anything he said or felt. Only the marks on his face concerned them. His surface.

After a pair of twelve-hour marathons with Cary and Johnson, my blood counts dropped again and my skin turned into something grey and gummy like newspapers left too long in the rain. I was losing the battle with this disease. Dying. And while it didn't feel good, mostly it didn't feel like anything at all. Days went by in the universe of my bed, waiting for the fevers to pass. When I was in the other place – it would be too much to say healthy – I looked for signs of contagion everywhere, like a collector of rare dolls. Would the smiling man at the grocery store make me sick? The bank teller? Their bodies were filled with a secret life that longed for new homes, their bacterial communions felt deeper and richer than small acts of conversation that provided only ground cover. When my tissues relented to admit the waiting fevers, I felt almost relieved. AIDS. When I found out, I was disbelieving. Acronyms couldn't hurt me, I thought. Now I was dying a little every day.

'Hi, Steve.'

'Hi, Auden. You look awful.'

Steve lacked the gift of the artful lie. It's not like he was condemned to tell the truth or anything, it just ran out of his mouth before he had time to order recalls. I knew he was worried I would die soon, but I felt that so long as he kept talking I would be able to hold on and recover. Some days I even wanted to get well.

Steve loved to talk, but even when he was on about microscopic life, or bowlers, or the scientific method, it all boiled down to love in the end. I couldn't stop listening to these stories, and he couldn't stop telling them. We had achieved something like symbiosis, and yes, Steve assured me, happiness was not an unknown quantity in the world of plants and minerals. We were not alone.

Even better, now that we had the painfully brief and not very satisfying sex thing out of the way (with that mild frisson of regret the body left behind, like an odour, to remind me: this wasn't the one and only, keep trying) the way was absolutely clear for us to build a new kind of playground. Despite the fact that Steve liked to leave his emotions where they belonged, on television, I found myself cozying up to his straight-man act.

'When I was younger I hardly spoke at all,' Steve assured me. 'As you might have guessed, many found this a winning design feature. Both men and women presented themselves to me, drawn by a silence they were powerless to resist. Now it feels like I'm talking all the time and attractions are increasingly difficult. The old rule still holds: the better people know you, the less likely that they will fall in love.'

I laughed until he started laughing with me, and I could feel some part of his inexpressible face flicker alive for a moment, as if our mutual hilarity offered him a consolation as rare and perfect as a knowing caress. Though perhaps, I had to admit, it was simpler than that, and he craved only an outlet for his prodigious musings. An audience. In either case, I was happy to oblige.

I don't know whether anyone else noticed, but the special features of my home entertainment centre have migrated inside my body. For instance, I never had recurring dreams until I bought a CD player with a repeat button. After that, there was no telling if the dream I was in would simply stutter away all night, caught in some neural loop learned from its new digital parents. After a lifetime of movie rentals and late-night television, most of my dreams came furnished with opening credits and a closing crawl, but this time it began without even the FBI copyright warning. In this dull dream, I had become a thick gummy substance that flowed briefly before settling, greyness on grey. I waited in this state for much of the night, and then a shiny trowel scooped me up and laid me onto a brick, and smoothed me flat, then laid another brick on top of me. The pressure seemed unbearable at first, but I slowly got used to it. More bricks were added on top, and I got used to that too. I was part of a house, cornering a new subdivision, each dwelling exactly alike. As I stared into the unchanging view, I could feel my new hardening surface enter all of my neighbours' housing, spreading across the freshly laid brick, sealing cracks and providing a firm bond.

This went on for about six hours, give or take a REM moment or two. A noise startled me awake, and in the ensuing confusion I reached for the bedside waterglass and somehow managed to punch it clear across the room. Was that my hand? It couldn't have been my hand, the old faithful that responded to every whim, no matter how frivolous.

I was still sweeping glass, which was busy dividing itself, like most everyone I know, into ever smaller versions of itself, when the door knocked and Steve walked in.

'When did you start coming right on in here?'

'When you stopped answering the door.'

He tucked a chuckle beneath his breath and settled down on my couch object. It was really just a couple of chairs the neighbours had worn to the frame and left for dead on the curb. I kissed them together with a foam slab and threw a blanket overtop. It was pretty comfortable.

'I see you're doing that thing with the glass again.'

'What thing?' I asked, looking up from a dustpan filled with nearly invisible shards. I would have to buy plastic glasses instead. But could I still call them glasses?

'That thing where you pretend that each piece of glass infinitely subdivides into smaller versions of itself.'

He took the dustpan and hung it up on a nail and motioned me towards the desk. No matter how little I moved I was covered in a fine sheen of sweat. He said that we were going to begin an experiment together, and I searched through a box of supermarket coupons to find a lonely pencil that would keep my wet hands company. The recycling bin yielded a sheaf of flyers that served as note paper. As he continued to lay a blanket of speech over everything, granting to even the most familiar of gestures (getting off the couch, scratching an itch) a nearly maternal comfort, Steve never used the words they preferred at the clinic, like *placebo* and *double blind studies*. It was only an experiment, he assured me, that's all. He was going to tell stories that would fill me like a plastic glass of water and slowly replace the narrative of illness with a healing alternative. Once finished, this writing would become part of some machine, but he was a little hazy on this point. While he spoke to me in the voice I had once thought of as my own, he made me write. I had to get it all down, he said, which was weird, to say the least. My writing had consisted mostly of shopping lists and signing cheques, but here I was staining pages with something like happiness. Or at least distraction.

'Where shall we begin?' he asked as I dutifully scribbled down his question. This was like being back at work with Johnson. I looked up into his patient eyes for more and realized he was waiting for me to conjure the rest. I wondered aloud. 'In high school?'

B ack in high school, in what he thought of as a 'pre-Steve' period, all Steve really wanted was to slip into the same MTV-inspired uniforms of his peers. Unfortunately, after a few vaguely prodding queries, he was led to understand that his democratic sexual interests (did it really matter if it was a boy or a girl?) were not generally shared, making him feel more lonely than ever. He had no hope and less interest in becoming popular. He wanted only to go unnoticed, to evade the punishing intelligence of his classmates, who hardly showed a pulse when it came to matters of math or history (the future was their home, not the past) but who sprang to collective life whenever they sensed an outsider in their midst, some unfortunate who could be manhandled by all those who felt the frustrations of growing old too slowly.

The mall became Steve's oracle of belonging. There among the overlit stacks of denim and impractical shoes lay every bit of camouflage he would ever need, if only he could overcome his natural inclination for the clumsy and stale-dated, the badly fitting uniforms of yesterday, the kitsch of generations not yet born. The remainder bins were a particular torment for him, filled with cast-offs devised by colourists who had exhausted every reasonable chroma and who had kept right on with lines no one could possibly be interested in. Except Steve.

On the Friday before his fourteenth birthday, he arrived still feeling the familiar divide between his need to belong and a quality he would learn to despise in the coming years, his taste. After an agonizing hour spent in the company of a salesman who was flattered by his attentions, he managed at last to leave the mall empty-handed. He had very nearly shelled out for a buckskin suit and bolero tie, which had appealed to the adventurer in him, and the fact that it had been tie-dyed lent it a certain cross-generational fascination he was eager to explore. But at the last moment he saw himself in the eyes of his classmates, and returned it with a heavy step to the dummy that had been wearing it. It was not the buckskin but his desire, his need, that made him feel more than ever the terrible separation between himself and those he was condemned to share his days with. Armed with this new proof of his unsuitability, he stumbled from the mall.

In his haste to leave, he took the first opening that offered itself, a side door rarely used, which opened onto a swarm of chess tables. Their patrons were aging still lifes counting out their fortunes on black-and-white concrete tiles. He must have passed them a hundred times without ever noticing. As he threaded his way through the players, he realized that each of them seemed quite alone, though unwilling to budge from a chosen side of the board. It was then he saw, following heads lifted in expectation, the small figure of a boy walking rapidly between them. He was no older than Steve: reluctant growths had begun to claim the adolescent chin, slim arms moved with a certainty that belied his years. He walked with a rooster stoop, jogged forward by subtle jerks of his head, which seemed to take in just about anything that didn't lie directly in front of him. In fact, the boy scarcely seemed to notice the chess pieces at all, looking out into the passing traffic for signs of his next move.

Steve stood confounded and confused. He had scoffed for years at Hollywood's crude messaging of love, the tricks of light and choreography that bent entire cities so that its primest cuts could life-mate after a single look. Imagine his surprise when he felt himself running short of breath at the sight of this nervously handsome prodigy. He had never even wanted a pair of shoes so much as this. The fact that a moment before they had been strangers meant nothing to him now. Sweat burst out of every available pore, turning him into a walking septic tank. He couldn't help it, whenever he got turned on he would get that smell on him so there could be no mistake. Of course he was mortified, and backed up against the nearest doorway in a pitiful state, hoping above all to be seen. Sure, the young genius was playing on a dozen boards at the same time, but was there any way he could fail to notice the hothouse of attention leaving foul pools on the sidewalk?

Gene made his way from one table to the next, nervously jabbing pawns across the board, slashing bishops and knights into his opponents' defences, until they conceded one after another. Pausing at each table to collect his modest wagers, and politely declining comment on the failed gambits of his older acolytes, he looked cornered for a moment, lost in the grey tide. He ducked and feinted his way towards the entrance of the mall where Steve was already waiting for him. He had prepared his opening line carefully, polishing it while the slim-hipped genius strode from board to board.

'I've never really cared about chess. Would you like to go get a drink?'

How could Steve have known that these were exactly the words his young charge had been waiting to hear? All his life Gene had been something of an aberration owing to his prodigious skills on the board, hanging out with older and older men, until his only companions were nearing the end of their days. He had begun to worry that he would lose the knack for middle age and grow from adolescence to senility, the only company left to him spirits returned from the big board in the sky to demand one more game on the speed clock. So Gene fell into step easily enough with Steve's shambling sense of misdirection, which finally took them to a watery-draft dive called Captains. Business here was always poor enough to ensure that no embarrassing questions about age or identification were ever asked, not when there was coin on the table. It was Steve's hip card, and he played it whenever he had the chance, though he hated drinking then. He would have really preferred a banana split or even a Creamsicle, but he'd never seen the big screen lit up with anything like Creamsicles, so he stuck to the draft, worrying it with unrehearsed fingers while he looked into its amber future.

'You know Paul Morphy?' Gene asked, demonstrating his premature beer etiquette. He kept lowering his head into the mug and pecking at it as if it were glued to the table.

'We've never met.'

'You wouldn't. He died a hundred years before you were born.'

'Wait, wait,' Steve urged, with a sudden illumination. 'This is a chess story, isn't it?'

'And your point is?'

'Nothing, no, go on. I'm transfixed.'

Transfixed was one of those magical words Steve imagined necessary to produce love. There were others, of course, like *providential* and *embosom*. Actually the list was quite long, though he was relieved to get *transfixed* out of the way so early in the conversation. Things were going well.

'Paul Morphy was the best goddamn chess player in the world.' Gene looked over at him then with his lower lip stuck out, ready for Steve's challenge, braced for the usual outrage about generations of overlooked Soviet grandmasters.

Instead Steve only shrugged, conceding Gene territory he'd worked all his life to claim. 'Paul Morphy.'

'Right. He beat every master in the world, sometimes playing multiple games blindfolded, and you know how he wound up? Arranging women's shoes in circles. Usually his mother's, but when he was still on the beam he would talk young women into visiting his flat and leaving behind their footwear.'

'He must have had an enviable collection,' Steve allowed, drawing some of the bitter draft up a nasal passage by accident.

'Of course there wasn't a pair that fit him,' Gene retorted.

'Of course,' Steve retorted back.

'For the last eight years of his life he always sounded ... ' Gene's voice trailed off and he seemed suddenly despondent, as if recalling the death of a childhood pet.

'Yes?' asked Steve.

'The way he sounded was always the same.'

Steve squared himself to face Gene, pausing to roll the cold glass over one cheek to ease the sweaty cascade. 'You mean Morphy said the same thing over and over.'

'Yes,' Gene admitted.

'Like a record player. Only record players don't cry.'

Gene looked through the far window as if into another time. 'His sister thought he was trying to explain his philosophy of chess, but his mouth could only form the same sentence. Again and again.'

'Until he died.'

'They were his last words.'

'Well, they would be, wouldn't they? Do you like women's shoes, Gene?'

'What?'

'Do you prefer women's shoes?'

'No, not at all.'

'Me neither. I guess we won't have to worry about *that*.'

Steve knew it was time for a move of his own, and lacking the experience, the rhetorical dexterity, he simply asked, 'Why don't we go to my place and take our clothes off and see what happens?'

'Just like that?' Gene replied, a little taken aback.

'No, no, please,' Steve tried to assure him. 'Finish your drink first.'

Steve looked up at me suddenly with a face that had lost its proportions, like he'd swallowed some of the furniture. 'I have to go now,' he announced and swam to his feet. No matter how many times he made his way towards the door I never saw him close it. He never left the room. He disappeared. I got up unsteadily and, leaning heavily on the almost-sofa, edged my way around it to the other end and then sat back down again. Soft spirals of colour turned around each ripple of the floor. My face and joints wouldn't be wetter if I'd been out in the rain, and I wondered if Steve thought I needed a recline before plunging any further into the knot of his teenage years. Or whether he'd taken a pit stop at the very moment of consummation, like those black-and-white love songs that carried movie lovers into the bedroom and then rushed past them for a long look out the window. There were some things that could not be put into words, though I suspected that they too, in time, would become part of the machine.

When Steve reappeared beside the bed with a pad of paper and a pencil, he had three faces, each wearing a primary colour. When I squinted, I could bring them together, and he appeared in full colour, but mostly it was too difficult, so I let the NBC peacock of his face hover across his narrow shoulders. I wanted to look out the window to get some idea of what time it might be, but he'd drawn the shade. Was it afternoon? After midnight? He waited until I settled the paper on my lap and then resumed his once-upon-a-times.

Soon Steve and Gene were inseparable, browsing the malls like two parts of the same secret, filling in each other's sentences, laughing at the same bad jokes, wondering that someone so funny and charming and lovely could have existed in this world after all. It even turned out that their parents had brought them to the same barber, who delivered the same annoying Gunther Cut, so named because it was a style designed to make its wearer deeply attractive – to someone living in, say, King Arthur's time. Today it was beyond hopeless, a helmet-like apparition that was part sheepdog, part Viking shield. Steve had dubbed his plumage Gunther because it made him look like one, and even though both he and Gene had been allowed the freedom of choosing their own barber for years, they continued to trudge back to the same scissors that had afflicted them as children, preferring a certain catastrophe to the untried dos lying in wait. The barber had other pictures on his wall to prove it, cuts so awful no one would dare venture outside, which is why they were never seen on the streets. Together, Steve and Gene made a pact. They would leave their old barber and, armed with a picture of Paul Morphy, a sullen-looking man already gone mad by the time the photo was taken, they decided to have their heads reshaped. Let others continue pilgrimages to Gunther. Freed in their new love, they were determined to resemble the world's once-greatest chess master.

Gene was a boy genius whose world-weary innocence and overly large forehead aroused an almost supernatural devotion on Steve's part. He could stare for hours at that forehead, watching the clockwork mind run through a network of small furrows and creases already beginning to show. Gene was a worrier, and so utterly lacking in guile that everything he felt was plainly written on his face. This delighted Steve no end, and provided an endless source of amusement, especially when Gene tried to lie, which was rarely, because he did it so badly, though Steve tried to encourage him. 'You should really try to lie more often,' he'd tell Gene, though in general he was reluctant to assume the declarative mode. Gene's attempts at untruth were accompanied by a volcanic face reddening, his eyes straining to escape the uncertain lure of mendacity. When caught out in the act of lying he became, for Steve at least, irresistible.

It was only a question of time before Steve took up the game of chess. Even replying to the simplest question, Gene liked to play his answers out on the board, and their mutual hilarity came to rely on an increasingly complex set of codes that cross-fertilized Morphy's championship matches with a Woody Allen joke book and a volume both considered the funniest book ever written, *The Tibetan Book of the Dead*. Steve was initially bewildered when Gene smiled to himself, half whispering, half thinking, 'Pawn to king four, king to bishop three, pawn to king five, pawn to bishop five!' But in no time at all he was swapping chess patterns with discerning mumbles of his own, goofing on new riffs with a beginner's alacrity.

Steve quickly attached himself to the intricacies of the Queen's Pawn Opening, stock opening for Bobby Fischer, the magus of recluse who once had all his fillings taken out before a match, fearing radio transmissions from his Russian opponents. Steve relived the Fischer-Spassky Rampage in Reykjavik, the Battle of Berne, the Siege of Sicily. While Gene favoured a strategy of all-out assault, no matter how poor his position, Steve inclined towards the counterpunch, allowing his opponents to overextend before sitting back to watch as they collapsed beneath their own weight. Steve had discovered the judo of chess. Designing ever more elaborate traps for his opposition, he understood the board as a mirror of its players. Unfortunately, his most usual companion at the board was Gene, and as the speed clocks wore down, their play shifted from a lopsided annihilation to slogging trench warfare, from studied counterattack to a mutual defensiveness. As Steve's game progressed, Gene's grew slowly worse, both feeling the wound of love heal over, leaving them each inured to the other's charms. It was just a matter of time.

They grew bored without being able to admit they hoped for anything else. Day after day, move after move, they were a little too young for happily-ever-afters. After high school, the Pirc-Modern, the Rat and the Nimzo-Indian were openings they shared only with others. One morning, or at least that's how Steve told it, Gene fell in with a big-boned girl who punched the clock with such force the hands spilled out of the glass, spun onto the board and pointed directly at him. *J'accuse*, they fairly screamed at Gene. *You are playing at love. Hiding behind the idea of feelings. With Steve you are only practicing a part while keeping yourself at one remove, always ready for chess, your one true passion. If you really loved someone you would give up the board, your days and nights would be filled with wanting them.* Of course these were ridiculous thoughts, but he was still a teenager, so he kissed her across the shattered remains of an impregnable variation on Botvinnik, and they left hand in hand, leaving Steve to finish the match with an irate barkeep. Steve was heartbroken: he had lost at one stroke his chess companion, his lover and his drinking partner. They spoke again only once, ten years later, meeting by chance at the baggage retrieval of the Schiphol airport.

'Oh, hi, Gene,' Steve said.

'Hi,' Gene replied, without really knowing who was addressing him. His eyes had grown worse as he got older, and though he knew he should get glasses he kept holding off, mostly out of vanity. He squinted through the fluorescent glare, recognizing at last that it was Steve. Steve Reinke. After all these years.

'Gee, hi, Steve,' Gene said, and immediately set off in search of a taxi. He knew that Steve had never believed in chance, but the prospect of resuming their former love held little charm for him. The truth was, Gene hardly remembered it. His past was a foreign country rarely visited. In place of memory there was only the vague feeling of shame. For Steve and Gene, there would be no second act.

'I think it's true what they say in all those songs: falling in love requires overvaluing the tiny ways in which one individual varies from another,' Steve assured me. We were sitting in Charlie's, right up at the counter so we could feel the bacon fat warm our cheeks. Did everyone here order bacon? Everybody but Steve perhaps, who couldn't bear to eat an animal so intelligent.

'A pig and a chicken were walking by city hall and noticed a big fundraiser for the homeless. Bands played as politicians were auctioned off and, caught up in the spirit, the pig suggested to the chicken they make a contribution. "Super," said the chicken. "Let's donate ham and eggs." "Wait a minute," said the pig. "For you that's a contribution. For me it's a commitment."'

He still couldn't resist the smell, though. He thought of bacon as incense, a heady brew promising sharp thoughts and sharper appetites. We'd come here so he could regale me with once-loves, but he wanted to make this one thing clear: 'The events of my past aren't the backstop for my pitching now.'

'No?' I asked him.

'No. They're part of the machine, that's all.'

I wanted to ask him if eating bacon was any way to learn about pigs, but he gestured impatiently to the block of paper where I'd been scribbling notes. He said we were making a machine together, only instead of throwing the switch or connecting wires, we just needed to sit in the bacon mist and keep laying words down like tiles in a bathroom. I picked up the pencil and waited for him to start again.

Steve eventually abandoned chess as a model of desire, unable to find a match where both players worked the same side of the board. In the ache of his despair, he returned to his earlier conviction that it was possible to fall in love with anyone, that love was a kind of machine that reflowed chemistry, immune-system response and patterns of speech until a correspondence, however temporary, became possible. He kept returning to the shipwreck scenario: if a ship ran aground on an island so remote it didn't even have cable TV, and only two crawled up out of the wreckage, wouldn't they eventually fall in love, no matter their allegiances, their likes and dislikes? Using the tools of sex and conversation, two unlikely pieces could be smoothed to fit more perfectly. But as Steve continued to date, mostly without great success, he began to conceive of a machine outside the human body that might become a vehicle for the most basic of human emotions. He bought his first video recorder hoping to make not another movie about love but a movie that would make love possible.

Like all great lovers, Steve turned towards himself before looking outside. He began making videotapes that abandoned the task of fact-gathering in order to change the attention of seeing itself. His four-hour close-up on a red handkerchief, for instance, offered its viewers the full lexicon of red, from the pale blush of a child's scrape to the red of Newton's apple. No one who saw it would ever experience colour in the same way again. He started creating time maps of key street corners in the city, compressing weeks of apparently random events into the blink of an eye, until they appeared as recognizable patterns. How else would we know how to run into exactly the person we needed to meet, unless we were already hip to the accidental, the chance encounter?

Steve's first subject in these experiments, his ur-viewer, was of course himself. He tracked the long hours of cathode exposure in a spiral-bound notepad, and while he didn't know it at first, this eventually became the book of his new personality. In just a few months he had left behind the complex orchestral scores of his childhood in favour of straight-ahead boy-band pop. His slouch straightened, the Wallabies were left behind. During walks that grew more and more frequent, he could eventually make out every blade of grass and every colour of shade beneath a tree, count the number of crickets in a night chorus. And with people it was just the same. When he was fully juiced he could look deep into the history of strangers just by hearing them say hello. There were some personalities so intense he could hardly stand beside them, though these were rare. Mostly he encountered grey zones of small worries that were easily dissembled beneath videos customized for their new audience. With his new tapes he hoped to show that anyone at all could undo the lifetime of habits we named as ourselves and experience the world as it really was, infinite.

Steve began a new series of screenings, going where no artist had dared to tread, the I'll-drink-to-that frat houses of the local university. While they were still condemned to fish for whales in puddles outside the cop shop, Steve's unstoried eye candy seemed just the thing to whip unsuspecting freshmen into helpless stupors of obedience. Steve divided his new audience into equal halves. The first would watch extremely short work, hours of footage compressed into a few seconds, while the other half would watch the same footage extended via slow motion for an entire day.

As it turned out, Steve's viewing sessions didn't last much past Frosh Week. The logic of frat-house belonging dripped away as watchfuls absorbed the two-hour movie of someone shovelling a driveway or the day-long slow-motion study of someone taking off his jacket. Each moment of the face could be read in these primal documentaries. Happiness and terror had been buried all along in the most ordinary activities, invisible until Steve offered his viewers time enough to notice. After stepping back into the wonder of their own lives, the noisy communion of the fraternity seemed a long way from heaven. Alarming drop-out rates soon led to emergency meetings and a rush to judgment: there would be no more videos permitted on campus.

David approached Steve after a screening, which was unusual. He had been in the slow-motion group, a lanky wide receiver with sure hands and a scholarship. Mostly people left Steve well enough alone – there wasn't anything of the star in his operation – but David was curious: there was something he recognized onscreen, and he had to meet its maker to be sure. They slipped off to Armitage Shanks, one of those unfortunate culinary ventures that divided its fare evenly between Chinese and Canadian food, ensuring a democracy of bad taste. Of course it was cheap and so was Steve. He had been eating there for years, alphabetically working his way through the menu. According to his unwavering schedule, he was due to order potato mash with baked beans, which would almost certainly cause problems in the gas department later. But when David began to talk, Steve lost all thought of dinner. They spoke all night, and by noon the next day they were still conferring, slowly bending from fatigue. At last, on their second night, they collapsed together on Steve's foldaway couch-bed, too tired to resist the obvious attraction, the mutual fascination, the happiness each held as a promise for the other.

Steve had never watched a football game, but was keen to accompany David whenever he played. Soon enough he started

designing videos that allowed his new charm to experience everyone on the field in slow motion, while David continued to move
at a regular clip. The ball appeared to him as a fat, achingly slow
target, and all of a sudden David was no longer a promising
rookie but an unstoppable one-man attack. Steve beamed on
with a kind of paternal satisfaction, though he grew increasingly
jealous of the elaborate end-zone celebrations. In full view of
hundreds, teammates thought nothing of rubbing David's cele-
brated butt, hugging him in joy or dancing together. The two of
them were a great deal more restrained at home. 'Do you have
to wear my jersey to bed?' David would ask him. 'I feel like I'm
taking advantage of myself.' Steve's incessant pleas for replay
fell upon ears already deafened with backside deceptions, counter traps and off-tackle draws.

Success quickly went to David's head, and then began to affect
other parts of his perfect body. But his season was triumphant,
and his finest moments were reserved for the championship
game. After launching a spectacular opening-kick return, he
seemed to float through defenders' hands, breezing past even the
quickest of cornerbacks on his way to record-breaking scores.
American scouts were in attendance and he accepted a handsome
scholarship to go south. Steve had already resigned himself to the
inevitable, and as a parting gesture of goodwill he made David a
present of the early tapes. Unfortunately these were left behind
in the rush out of town, and David soon found himself running
average routes on an ordinary field before being asked to sit on
the bench. Even without Steve's video steroids, the view from
the sidelines must have made the game appear slower than ever.

Steve took the pencil out of my hand and laid it on the milk-
crate bedstand. 'That's enough for today,' he said without

speaking a word, and I sank back into the forever relief of the pillow. The feeling of no feeling at all, as if I didn't have a head. Could any lover offer me pleasures as reliable as this pillow?

'Some machines are made of steel or plastic, this one needs only words,' he told me, and I reached again for the pencil, but he took my hand and held it, assuring me that I'd remember later. 'As we get deeper into it, you'll start noticing changes.'

'What kind of changes?'

'The words that live inside you will start to shift. Right now these words are gathered in patterns, like the kind of templates that collect to form your skin or your immune system. You can think of them as wallpaper if you like. All we're doing now is stripping the house.'

'And then?'

'Time for a new look. It's going to feel good, I can promise you that.'

'What happens if we don't put up new wallpaper?'

'Without any words left inside, I guess you wouldn't be able to tell anybody about it.'

Steve's calm voice released each exposure of his past in equal measures, there was no sweetness in his storytelling, nor hints of revenge. Maybe there was no room for it in the machine, perhaps it was exactly feelings of this kind that would cause fatal imbalances, like a recipe with the wrong quantities. How carefully he spoke in order to put together this delicate machine of words, I thought, welcoming again the drowsiness that invariably accompanied my pillow companion. The room flickered for a moment, then grew dark and quiet. It was the middle of the afternoon, but the dark suggested midnight.

When I woke, the bed was clinging from night sweat, the sheets so wet I wrung them out in the tub. I towelled off and swapped them for fresh, snapping the overly large ground-sheet away from me again and again for the simple pleasure of seeing the long white cotton unfurl. I mitred the corners and added layers, tucking and folding, wondering if others would notice any kind of difference once the machine took hold inside. Would I gain the snug glow that strangers exhibited after eating meals in Paris or witnessing miracles in Rome? Could I look forward to waiting in lines, having conversations with strangers in elevators, throwing myself out of airplanes for sport?

The phone rang and the phone hadn't rung for a long time. Like the extra pairs of throwaway chopsticks or the hood ornaments for cars I would never own, the phone had become part of my apartment's forgotten inventory, so when the bell sounded I couldn't help barking in surprise, 'What do you want?' I was greeted with an earful of static, and then a ghost voice that promised shiny vacations and a subscription to a newspaper over-achieving kids couldn't give away in the mall.

The same dream waited for me sleeping or awake. I am Betty McGlown, one of the four original members of the Supremes. Whenever I sing the word *love* with my girls from the Brewster-Douglass projects, each member of the audience falls in love with the first thing they see after leaving the show. Because most of our gigs are in downtown Detroit, catastrophic numbers of young teenagers have become smitten with fire hydrants and parking meters. In order to save the city, I have been asked to leave the group. This morning, the dream stuttered and stopped as the phone bleated from its cradle. I touched my feet to the floor and they were my feet again, and I watched as they took me all the way to the bathroom. Small miracles.

The phone rang again and I shuffled back to the bed and picked it up. The vacation voice started in, and this time I didn't hang up, savouring the promise of every word. I wanted to hear it all.

During the week, Steve was a phantom in his own body, a cube prole booking gigs for a jazz singer named Sonora Williams. 'Well, Sonora Williams would like ... ' 'Sonora Williams needs ... ' Her talent, unfortunately, would never quite reach the heights of her ambition. Nonetheless, there were a thousand bars in this province alone, so each Monday he began the long call sheet, his mouth glued to the phone, his fingers a combination of keypads and fax lines, spreading his singer's two-octave range across the land like the fingers of an oriental fan. The job was clearly a tweener, better than dishing up burritos at La Ha, but not as good as high-concept tire commercials. Steve figured it wouldn't be long before his restless video production found its way to market. Soon, he assured me, even our most private thoughts would be turned into money. It was just a question of time.

He spoke about his job exactly once, and never mentioned it again. He didn't want his work becoming him, turning him into something, anything really, that might take him away from his art. Or his desire, which he insisted was really the same thing. Every Friday night, after the dinner special at Armitage Shanks, his body returned to him, and he began his second life whose only allegiance was to the weekend. Steve liked to visit the Shaft, because despite its name and a paint job that looked like someone had to leave in a hurry, it was a pretty cosy place, filled with easy-listening couches and play areas. And there was no dress code, not like at the Crypt, where it was leather only please or, worse, at Ollie's where they didn't wear anything at all. That was fine if you were under thirty, only nobody at Ollie's was under thirty, which is why they drank too much.

One night he crossed the threshold (others made their way through doors, Steve crossed thresholds) and paused to take in the empty setting. He liked to come early and choose from a maximum set of possible vantages. The right chair made him feel like the director of this particular love cruise. While the after-dinner crowd mustered, he had a drink and then another before he spotted the blond man-boy wearing a scratched-up pair of bell-bottoms and cowboy boots and nothing else. He had a kisser so large and red that it looked like it would never stop opening, it just went on and on until his face ended. It was a mouth used to settling scores, only Steve didn't catch this right away. No one did.

'Buy you a drink?' Steve asked.

'Why not?' replied the stranger.

'Steve.'

'Jody.'

Giving away nothing. They strolled towards the bar with the X-ray machine set on low impact and took the first round standing. By the second, Steve was in love.

'Let's go.'

'Sure.'

They kissed. Jody bit him hard on the lower lip, and every trace of Steve's working life disappeared. They headed back to his apartment, a one-bedroom homage to the seventies, where Jody made him wait, keys in the door, and sucked him hard, his pants down on the welcome mat. Miraculously, no one appeared, though Steve thought he saw the neighbour's spy hole darken. He was tied, licked, fucked, and all night Steve asked himself: how did he know I wanted this? It was only after, sharing a nightcap of vodka martinis, that he noticed the small raised marks on Jody's ankles, no bigger than subway tokens. Kaposi's sarcoma.

I called Johnson with a voice reduced to a throaty whisper, which he understood as shorthand for contagion. Before ringing off, and granting me the largesse of another week in the paradise of my sickbed, he made me spin a story about a patently fabricated encounter I'd had the night before with a bedwetting speed-metal guitarist. At least I didn't have to surrender to apologies. 'We're counting on you!' he said, already distracted moments after I finished the narration, and I assured him I was counting too.

Each day I worked a little on the machine. Steve told me that, like any factory-made confection, this one didn't begin at the beginning. He assured me that the big picture would reveal itself if I kept laying down the next word. Turning the page.

Steve is what they call a video artist, which is kind of like making television for one viewer at a time. Steve called television 'the poor boy's heroin,' which didn't stop him from watching, of course, and he didn't mind that his own signals were more modestly distributed. Steve understood that the circulation of power had little to do with how visible anything was. His most important works were never seen by anyone. What he showed instead were his outtakes, the moments when he left his camera running by accident. These were more than enough. The first tape of his I ever saw was a short trip, a few minutes long maybe, no more, and when it was over I had learned a whole new way to smile. All I retained was its humour, the colour green and, of course, the grain of that magnificent voice. I longed to return, and began a daily pilgrimage to a little-known gallery in a despised part of town, performing a task I had not indulged since grade school, committing a text to memory. My memory was digital, it was either on or off. I remembered everything or nothing at all. But I was determined to hold on to this rap. The text of what turned out to be the first of *The Hundred Videos*.

Like everyone else, I wanted to do something on AIDS, a close, personal look at a man dying. Wanting the work to be as effective a documentary as I could manage, that is, as visceral as possible, I would want to include my subject's death. In fact, the video would not be complete without his death. So I set out in search of a subject. These were my initial parameters. In order not to confuse issues: a white, anglophone, homosexual male, and for added empathy, he should be under thirty. Due to budget restrictions, I would prefer one who would die six to eight weeks after taping began, yet would be strong enough in the initial days of taping that I could record his basic life story. What I had in mind seemed fairly simple. The audience would construct an image of him, even as he himself wore away. I'd need some home movies, but if my subject didn't have any, another's could be used. Everyone's home movies are basically the same.

This became my problem. As my search continued, I began imagining with increasing specificity the things I would like my subject to say and do. The longer my search took, the more specific my criteria became. And the more specific my criteria, the more difficult, and therefore longer, my search. It seemed an unending spiral, two sets that might never overlap. Even if there were specific points of juncture, how could I find the individual that would be at each one? My project risked degenerating entirely.

Was it because I was so recently diagnosed that I found this tape so fetching? Steve had managed to convey, somehow, everything I might ever say about this inscrutable intruder, which had already forced me to accept, as the radical root of my new personality, the very thing that was bent on killing me. Steve's tape offered me the only possible solution. Fiction.

Sometimes I missed Dr. Phil the way a boy missed his father. How very close the world appeared when he was on television, much closer than the neighbour's tambourine practice or the passing thunder of footsteps down the hallway as kindergarten tyrants chased down their latest plaything. I gathered up the small moments that remained in memory and pressed them into the place where my life used to be. Not knowing whether I had enough of what it took, whether I even wanted to. There, I'd said it. And now I'd always say it. *Whether I even wanted to.* Whether I even wanted to live.

There were drugs waiting. The script was already written by a doctor so filled with kindness he smelled like sugar when I went to see him. No one ever died in this candy factory. But I didn't want to jump into the medicine, and as the weeks went on, this made him impatient, though he masked it with concern. Like James Brown, the doctor believed everyone had a good thing inside them. 'It's for your own good thing,' he assured me. But drugs were a further admission that this illness was part of me and inescapable, and I wasn't ready to say yes to that yet. Not just yet.

I longed to do nothing, make no decisions, pretend it didn't happen. But the doctor kept pushing. 'If you don't take these medicines ... ' he began, and then his voice trailed off. There were certain words he couldn't pronounce, maybe they were against the code or something. What he wanted to say was, 'You're going to die.' What he tried to tell me was, 'You're going to die, and these drugs will make us feel we're doing something. Why won't you help me?'

Dr. Phil is counselling the Manns, an overweight couple with a homely thirtysomething daughter who still lived at home. After persistent exposure, they had become characters in their favourite television programs, but because they all inhabited different shows, no one got along. The mother felt particularly resentful because she was usually cast as the studio audience and didn't get any lines, which meant no talking in the house. After a series of gruelling confessionals, Dr. Phil arrived at a pleasing solution. The family would no longer inhabit roles, but the staging of those roles. The father became Camera One, the mother the teleprompter, while the daughter took on the role of the script doctor. All of a sudden they were busy producing their own version of an American family, feeling like they belonged. Dr. Phil concluded, 'The beauty of the world may be all around us, but sometimes it is hard to spot.'

Sometimes Steve liked to come over and watch the stock channel. He wasn't an investor or anything, he just loved to see the numbers move. They had an uncanny rhythm that he hummed to himself as the interminable scroll ran past. Steve said the Exchange, the DOW and the NASDAQ all had a shape, they were filled with patterns of continuity and order. It was like watching a thousand people perform intricate stitching at the same time, their small, skillful hands flying across the fabric, weaving in and out of each other's threads. What never failed to keep him glued to the set, hour after hour, is the way this design kept its secret. Because it was everywhere at once, it was hard to see. It was there all the time, right up front, so it was overlooked. We were, all of us, a part of this Exchange, our small movements of opening and closing summarized in its flow charts. Steve said that we were so attached to our alternations of chance and routine moments we never managed to see beyond them, towards the far shore of capital, and ourselves.

Like the deep shape of the Exchange, Steve also longed to be invisible, and in order to embrace his new-found cause more deeply he decided to join *The Lofters*, a local reality-TV program. He wanted to be on television because that way he figured he would be truly unseen. I didn't catch the logic at first. I imagined that being on television would make him more noticed than ever, but he assured me it was just the opposite. 'Look, babe. People watch movies. And art. But not television. Television just fills up the place where your eyes go. People might seem familiar on the box, but you never really remember them once they're off-screen. TV helps us forget.'

The application form for *The Lofters* was modest, asking perfunctory questions about his age and height and preference in pets. What really counted was the video, which Steve knocked off in an afternoon, without really trying. It wasn't fair to the others, the ones who strained and worried over their audition tapes. Steve had been auditioning all his life for this part, the part of Steve Reinke, so when the tape arrived, the show's producers called right away and told him, 'YOU'RE A LOFTER NOW, STEVE!'

He was reluctant to share with me the small video he produced that finally opened the door to television, but at last, after some particularly animated nagging, he said that he would relate the incident that inspired him. I took up my pencil and waited, feeling not only my own anticipation, but the hope of the machine.

When my father died I was sad for a while, but I thought that would be that. I was already an adult and had no reasonable expectation of needing his presence in the future. One afternoon I was sitting in a shopping mall and overheard someone telling a joke. It was a joke I remembered my father telling and I associated it with him. I could not understand how someone could possess a piece of my father and unknowingly carry it around. I was jealous of this stranger who owned a piece of my father while I was left with nothing. Then I realized that the joke is a mechanism that allows language to wrap itself around an individual, creating and defining him. So when I present this joke to you, I'm not presenting a memory or impression of my father. I am presenting you with my actual father.

A man gets a new job and every day when he walks to work he sees, through the window of a house, a woman hitting a little boy with a loaf of bread. This goes on for many months. One day he sees the woman hitting the boy with a chocolate cake. He steps up to the window, unable to resist. 'Every morning I see you hitting this little boy with a loaf of bread. Why are you using a chocolate cake now?' 'Well,' the woman replied, 'today's his birthday.'

On his way over to the first day of the show, Steve stopped by to ask how he looked, though I think he was more concerned with how I looked. He probably learned these useful reversals during those grandmaster chess replays with young Gene. He was wearing a shirt that used to be an unnameable shade of yellow before it gave up the idea of being a colour at all, and it looked like it could fit at least one other person inside its ballooning polyester, two more in a pinch.

'I love it!' he announced proudly. 'Entire weather patterns circulate inside the shirt. The unusual volume permits warm and cool currents to meet.'

'But doesn't that produce rain?' I asked, still in a bed-bound stupor.

'Yes, but I'm getting used to that. Inside us, our bodies are in a state of continual irrigation. I am hoping for a symmetrical response in order to achieve a unity of inside and out.'

The ripening of his beloved fabric didn't worry him, and besides, if the producers refused it, Wardrobe would come up with alternatives. Not so secretly, he longed to lose himself in the wardrobe department, where new selves waited on every hanger.

He didn't mention Jody. He never said the words *Kaposi's sarcoma*, though every time I saw him it was on the tip of my tongue where it melted away, one smooth syllable at a time. Let him have his Lofters, Jody would be waiting for him when he got back. Or at least the consequences, the afterburn, of Jody's instant-breakfast happiness. It was hard to admit there was time, that *later* meant anything but tomorrow or, at the furthest stretch of the word, the weekend. But perhaps that was changing too.

'Good luck, Steve.'

'Good luck yourself. I'll come back and tell you the whole story.'

'I'm counting on it.'

JD called to pass along a rumour that the origins of the virus belonged to CIA experiments between animals and humans. Apparently one of the Pentagon brass had turned up positive and ordered the release of documents that would make a cure inevitable. He spoke in a breathless whisper, but when he got to the part about the cure, even JD couldn't help laughing. Please excuse me, I have to go walk across the lake now. Oh, could you hold on a minute? I just have to turn my tap water into beer. And don't worry your little head about Jorge. He's only resting now. I'm going to raise him from the dead before the guests arrive.

Steve never got to wear his yellow shirt on the show, but that was his only disappointment. Steve loved the Lofters and the Lofters loved Steve. There was Margie, the distress queen who was so beautiful she never had to talk, but under Steve's promptings she began to speak compulsively, and badly, to everyone around her. There was Bill, the slightly overweight hipster who had a secret affair with Steve while dating June, who was still recovering from the tragic car accident that killed both her parents and left her paralyzed from the waist down. Steve was older than most of them, but no one could really tell. The long hours he had put into being unnoticed paid off in the age department. He fit right in, and couldn't imagine a life better than this, with their fully accessorized loft, all expenses paid, cameras ready to record their every move.

Slowly, as the weeks went by, Steve seduced them all, one at a time, in alphabetical order, as it turned out, though no one realized this until later. He even managed to have sex with June, the woman in the wheelchair, who discovered through Steve's patient ministrations a new site of intense erotic pleasure, a kind of second clitoris located in the small of her back which was capable of producing devastating multiple orgasms. It was his voice, of course, no one could resist the allure of that siren's call. While having sex, he didn't touch her all over, but he talked, he spoke to each part of her body, and then all of their bodies, reawakening in them pleasures undreamt by those who had never been on television.

None of this was taped, the producers were careful never to show even casual nudity. The sponsors might revolt, and they could lose their hard-earned spot on prime time. All too soon, the Lofters found it hard to do anything if the camera wasn't there recording. Some were already constipated. But network prohibitions never deterred Steve. Unbeknownst to the crew, as soon as they turned their cameras off, he turned his on. He taped the Lofters asleep or peeing or vomiting during hangovers. In short, he made a catalogue of everything the producers were unwilling to show. He taught the Lofters how to use his little digital camera, which was so simple and compact they could record themselves when he wasn't around. They had become slovenly and unwashed until Steve began taping. Then there was a reason to shower again. Because someone was watching.

Just before the show's finale, Steve began assembling the gathered material. He started with the highlight reel, prepared to make a gripping, behind-the-scenes account. It should offer a withering critique of mainstream voyeurism while being sentimental and melodramatic in the same breath. Then he decided to throw all that away, because the beautiful takes, the flash, were never all that revealing. The real juice was the in-between moments, when nothing happened, or else those private encounters when the body spoke in spite of itself. After a few hours of mindful pruning, he was left with their sex scenes, which, he'd hardly realized at the time, all involved Steve. Somehow, over the last few weeks, no one in the loft had managed to have sex without Steve being present, even if he was only watching. He subdivided each act into its component parts: the caress of language, the initial genital contact, the graceless shedding of clothes. Through careful editing he joined each like-minded moment, collecting the exquisite uncertainty of one first touch after another, faces dissolving in shudders of release, the soft petition for more answered by another that sounded just the same. When he was done cutting, he waited for the show's three-hour finale, which would be broadcast live. Ignoring the producer's request for a last game of Twister, Steve played his tape while the Lofters looked on, at first in horror, then in stunned amazement. Here they were, caught in the act of love, and no one could tell one from another. They had the same expressions, used the same words, were delivered to exactly the same kind of happiness. They had become interchangeable. Parts of the machine of Steve Reinke.

In my new dreams I savoured dinners with conversation so witty my guests ached with laughter, and all of them begged me to share their bed afterwards, startled by my perfect fashion sense and sexual athleticism. Shallow dreams, I knew, but sometimes even the unconscious gets tired of outputting Greek myths and new corporate logos. Meanwhile, in my waking hours, a small, angry man with a mouth in place of understanding hunted for blame. Like the hummingbird, he'd learned just one tune, and never tired of playing it. It was my fault. That's what he let me know. Even if the day hadn't started up yet, something somewhere was going wrong and I was to blame. When I spoke too frequently, this feeling would start creeping into conversation. Some were born with subliminal seduction, others with subliminal failure: it was a little trick some of us had learned to keep happiness from spoiling a view that had grown only too familiar.

There were two things I knew for sure when I tested positive. That I was going to die. And that I was going to hunt down the voice that was forever busy inventing new kinds of failure, and squeeze its little windpipe until it snapped between my fingers. I would not die guilty. I just didn't have the time.

Steve stood against the window of my apartment, a dull blank, a silhouette. Behind him, Lake Ontario waved hello and good-bye in the same tailwind. He found a reassuring anonymity in the midday glare, when he was the darkest object in the room. He usually stopped by on the way from the show. Unlike the program's American counterparts, he and the rest of the cast were free to regain their usual vices in the off-hours, meeting up again in the morning fresh from what some show members had begun to call 'the other network.' What he had carefully walked around until this afternoon was any mention of his one-night love, Jody. The man-boy with the mouth that went on and on until he'd swallowed up a city of AIDS without knowing a thing about it.

'Of course we were using protection, Auden,' he told me. 'After all, it was our first date.'

'The way you described his Houdini act in the hallway: the belt, the slip knot, blindfolded with your own Calvins. Maybe there was a moment with Jody when you couldn't be sure ... '

'Maybe there was.'

He paced off the living room again and I watched him back and forth in even steps. He was counting prime numbers again, sending some irresistible backbeat of calm deep into his cell structure. I wanted him to stop anything from ever happening to me again, even as I searched his face for signs. Was it already there? Had the conversion already happened, was the system compromised, the blood already turned against itself? I looked at him the way parents might watch their child leaving home for the first time. *Please don't die before me.*

'Maybe there was,' he allowed.

He stared back at me with the same calm rolling off his face. He hadn't been careful exactly, but you didn't fall in love being careful. It was funny to see him like this, in love and all, or at least in the grip of a full-blown memory crush. Mostly Steve fell in love with ideas, which he embraced with an infinite care and delicacy. Books had long ago replaced people in his hierarchy of importance. But for every shelf of important poets and new world scientists there had been affections of devastating intensity, often involving people he might have kissed once in a bar lineup at the Shaft, or who walked out of the corner of one eye as he stood waiting to get change at the laundromat. Some, he was nearly embarrassed to admit, he had never actually spoken to, or even touched. But the mention of a name, the recall of an insolent bicep, even a coffee stain on a table might be enough to raise the terrible spectre of longing once more. And each time it happened he announced, with all the cheer of the BBC voice charged with reciting the time to the nearest minute, 'I'm in love.'

'Jody's a computer programmer for a graphics place back of Mutual Street. And of course he's not gay, not really, he wants to get married and raise monsters. But in the meantime it's hard to say no. I guess that's what love is sometimes. Saying no. So when I asked him how long he'd been positive, he set his drink down and left. Like it was my fault for telling him.'

'I can't believe he didn't recognize the signs. Not that far gone.'

'He didn't want to know.'

'I'm sorry, Steve.'

I walked him over to the couch and held him until the tears came. Because his new love was dying and he might never see him again. And if he did there would be another round of visits to the hospital, only he would be on the receiving end, weighing the friends who stopped coming by against the new ones, the ones who could smell the end and wanted to rub up against it a little bit, hoping to get lost in something larger than themselves. Killing with their kindness.

We decided that he would go to the clinic and take the test just to be sure. Some small crazy part of him thinking that if he came up positive he could find Jody again and share the oldest dream of the body. That we are not alone.

'It's so dark in here,' Steve complained as he groped his way to the light switch.

'I thought you liked it in the shade,' I replied, laughing as he bounced along the walls.

'I like it dark at night and sunny in the day. I could never be an Eskimo. If I were a teenage Eskimo, I'd go out on a Friday night and start drinking and I wouldn't stop until springtime. It's so much easier here. When the sun comes up you know it's time to go home.'

Steve's face was mercifully free of the disappointment that most brought to the door. Must you? Die here? In front of me? I hadn't been so fine lately, my small nagging cough turned into pneumonia, and after a hasty trip to the hospital, specialists put me on a respirator and everyone breathed easier. There would be another night after all, another visit from the doctor, and now, another from Steve. I didn't like company when I was on the mend because the illness got stuck in their eyes, so even if I got better it appeared only as a respite, a moment before dying. The end seemed a little further away when I was alone.

'Which gives the piggy bank more pleasure?' Steve asked me as he swept up a pile of last night's dishes into the sink. 'The insertion of individual coins in the little slotted notch of its head, or the unplugging of its bottom hole to let them all drop out together?'

'What about the slow build of pressure as the coins collect in its hollow gut?' I wondered.

'Hadn't thought of that,' he allowed.

Steve carried a couple of martinis back into the room, leaving a thin trail of liquid behind him. He liked to keep pouring until the booze hit the imaginary line running across the very top of the glass. In other words, he overfilled, ensuring that the slightest movement in any direction would cause spilling. No one managed his cocktails without a bit of awkwardness, including Steve himself, who found reassurance in this clumsy solidarity.

'It's funny, just in the last few days, I've stopped having dreams about the end of the world,' Steve announced cheerily, balancing his drink on a coaster tattoo inscribed on his forearm.

'I didn't know it was such a regular part of the menu.'

'You mean you've never ... '

'No,' I had to admit to him.

'Not even once?' he asked again, slightly incredulous.

'The world never ends in my dreams. Only I do.'

Moments like these were common with Steve. It had never occurred to him that his nighttime reveries weren't shared with others who lived on his frequency. Dreams were like television, or so he thought, nightly broadcasts viewed in a customized form we named the unconscious. Steve put the martini down and eyed me with a certain suspicion. Was it really possible I didn't dream about the world's end? Didn't the firebombing of Tokyo occupy at least as much cranial space as the location of good sushi restaurants?

'Okay. You're in a supermarket and you're looking all over for Oreo cookies when suddenly you spot them in the freezer section. The freezer section? Taking a quick peek around to make sure no one's got you on the radar, you crack open the bag and throw a couple back into your mouth. Taste endorphins flood your receptors. You have just been introduced to cookie royalty. Not only do they go down smooth, but the sharp, sugary aftertaste that makes you eat one after another to put off the bad feeling doesn't happen at all. Oreos, it turns out, really do belong in the freezer. Happier than you have any right to be, you pop the bag in your cart, when the alarm goes off.'

'An alarm in a grocery store?' I wondered aloud, thinking that I really did need to get out more.

'You're following me, right? The Oreos are in your cart when the alarm goes off, which means the big one's coming your way, the bomb of bombs, but because of advances in distant early warning you've got two, maybe three entire minutes before the whole city blows up. So what do you do next?' Steve settles back on his heels like some old frontier sheriff who has just laid down aces in the last hand of the night.

'Well, I've already had the Oreo cookie, so that's probably out. On the other hand, I could eat the whole bag and not feel overdone later because I guess there is no later, right? I can do anything I want and not feel guilty about it. Take my clothes off and curl up in the broccoli. Recite the Communist Manifesto backwards. I don't know what I'd do. Plant a wet one on the cute checkout clerk.'

'That sounds nice.'

'I can't believe you go over and over this stuff.'

'All my favourite people are dead,' Steve assured me, nodding earnestly in time to some inner beatbox. He didn't look sad when he said it. On the contrary, because the number of the dead far outweigh the number of the living, he had many friends to choose from. The libraries, for instance, were filled with them, and I'd seen him walk into reading rooms overcome with emotion, like someone arriving for a family reunion.

'But, Steve,' I had to remind him, 'you never actually met those people. You've only read their books. They could have been assholes.'

'They don't read like assholes. And besides, personality is highly overrated.'

Most of Steve's engagements, his emotional life, his heat, rested with the dead. There were a few composers (though he preferred the big pop sound of the nineties), a painter or two, but mostly it was writers. Steve lived inside the books he encountered; he threw himself between the covers knowing that soon there would be no one left to read them. Oh sure, someone would always be able to pick up a book and go through the motions, twitching over miles of letters all lined up in a row like a firing squad. But to really read a book was to feel it as an echo of all the books written before it, and more than that, to find inside its pages evidence of a life lived in words, as strange and rare as the frozen remains in Pompeii. If there was a sadness in this love, it was because he knew the videotapes he made with such abandon hastened the end of the book, or if not the book itself, then reading, which amounted to the same thing in the end. It was difficult for him to open a book without a sense of accusation, of outrage even, coming from the volume itself, pained to be handled by someone who had dedicated his life to destroying the thing he loved. This much was certain: Steve's video work was hastening the end of the book. And no one could have been more apologetic than Steve himself, who was the author of every book he read.

I arrived at the overcrowded corner ten minutes early, but Steve was already there, nervously drawing on a cigarette. Whenever he got really unstrung, he started drinking coffee, pots of black-beaned swamp mix from Colombia, which he swore was the only thing that really relaxed him. His body responded in waves of convulsive shudders that we both pretended not to notice. His seizure impressions allowed a clean metre perimeter around him, even on that busy corner. He appeared like a traffic jam all rolled up into one car, and I was surprised to see relief overtake his features when I walked into view.

'You're early,' Steve announced.

'You're earlier,' I shouted back from across the road, jumping the light ahead of a woman who seemed to be made entirely of elbows. When I got up in front of him, he nearly turned on his heel, but I caught a corner of his windbreaker and turned him and gave him a hug.

'Let's go upstairs.'

I always arrived at the clinic faintly cheered, feeling that none of its fatal deliberations could touch me anymore. Besides, it boasted the city's most comfortable waiting room. The furnishings were donated by none other than Mr. Mattress, the Bedroom King, who had turned his attention in recent years to the oversized butts of his favourite clients. He'd devised a line of couches as exquisite as his beds, so when we got there I sank into the deep end and let the foam layers work their magic.

'Why do they have to make it feel so good before it feels so lousy?' Steve wondered aloud.

We were just there to get the test. The results wouldn't come back for another week or two, so Steve wasn't really nervous, although all that coffee had him chatting up the overworked receptionist and anyone else he could get a word into. He sounded like someone calling a horse race. He just couldn't get the words out fast enough. 'You-know-there's-more-chickens-in-the-world-than-human-beings?-Twelve-million-more-in-fact-and-because-of-the-new-steroids-they're-poised-to-make-an-evolutionary-leap!-While-leaders-worry-about-the-price-of-the-baht-the-yen-the-dollar-the-revolution-is-coming-from-the-farm.'

'The revolution is coming from the farm!' he exclaimed again, as if his life depended on it, and maybe it did. Reception shot him a look over the phone, which hadn't stopped ringing since we arrived, and I peeled Steve off the ceiling tiles and made him sit down beside me. Maybe his perma-shudders hadn't been brewed after all, but resided in his new chicken-heavy diet. Like everyone else I knew, he was convinced the papers were filled with lies, only he couldn't stop searching for clues, reading between the lines for some moment of truth that had escaped the celebrity glare. This week it was chickens.

'A sudden jump in protein consumption is much more significant than a change in government or a declaration of war!' Steve announced loudly, though I was sitting close enough to count the hairs in his ears. 'We're looking through the wrong end of the telescope!'

I could only nod, and then a slight, balding man appeared from one of the closed doors. He didn't look like much, dressed down in civilian togs, but every step seemed to leave impressions in the wall-to-wall. One of today's docs. He looked young enough to be hurt by all the death in the room, and the fact that he was on the dealing end didn't seem to make it easier. 'Mr. Stanley?' he asked, and we both turned towards a twentysomething crossing over to the desk. Mr. Stanley just stood there a moment, wondering if maybe in that avalanche of paper they'd shuffled someone else's name in place of his own, swapped numbers in the blood labs, but knowing at the same time that hope was a thing of the past, already banished before he'd taken the long climb into the clinic. If he'd tested positive, only the formalities were left. Just before the door closed behind them, Steve followed some ghost trail of the boy who appeared to us both like a premonition of disaster. And then at last I could feel Steve relax. The whole cinched-up pressure of the room dipped a notch, because this was as bad as it got and at least we'd seen it now. When his turn came, Steve sat up with something like a smile. He was ready.

Steve emerged from the door of the blood room with a perfect calm settled over his face. The unknown was no longer a stranger to him. He paused for a moment at the desk, weighing an invisible reflection. Later he confided that he wasn't sure if he should leave a tip or something, not that he had change to spare, but everyone had been so nice and all, so damned cheery in the face of the unthinkable. Instead he turned, in a grotesque version of a pirouette (the only class he'd ever failed at school was gymnastics), and announced, 'We're leaving!'

Steve ejected out of the clinic and I fell in behind him as we made our way east, charging hard. He was usually not much of a walker, not after the invention of the car, the bus, the scooter.

'Auden, one day the humble scooter will make feet extinct!'

His feet scarcely stopped to touch the ground as he flung himself across the city. I kept looking for signs that the anxieties of a futureless future had taken hold of him, but nothing crossed the projection scrim of his face except the determination to keep moving. Though I'd seen enough of my friends grant Academy-calibre performances of themselves, outshining any star in the firmament sans drugs thank you very much, only to collapse a few weeks later in a retiring heap of self-loathing and fear. Fear is what got us all in the end. Good times were just another of its manifold faces, happiness a prelude to the inevitable descent. So I held an extra-keen watch on my charge, wondering if he would slip and panic and crumble like all the rest. My hope that he wouldn't was tied somehow to the feeling that Steve would find a way through, armed with his art and this new machine he insisted we were building together.

If he could make it, well then maybe so could I. As we slugged our way east with our tourist faces on, not heading anywhere in particular, the following four thoughts occurred to me:

1. I must have a Colombian double espresso *now*.
2. Unlikely as it seems, I have never had an espresso.
3. Never mind double.
4. Never mind Colombian.

But the voice inside my head, Steve's voice, insisted that only a Colombian double espresso would do. I had only heard this voice recite mystery books and shopping lists. It was my reader's voice, but now it had struck out on its own. Was this love? Had I never experienced the full flush of an emotion exhaustively described in Top 40 hits and after-school specials? Had some final resistance broken down and allowed me to experience the fullness of this emotion at last? But no. Steve was shaking his head back and forth even as we braced our way into a sudden gust, which made him look like a windup toy with a glitched chip.

'Steve, your voice, the voice I hear when I'm reading ... '

'Yes?'

'I hear it all the time now.'

'I know.' *How does he know?* 'We went over this last night.' He looked at me expectantly, but what was last night? Last night was laundry and that bad Margaret Cho movie. Or was it peanut-butter pancakes and the bad Demi Moore movie?

'You don't remember, right?' he asked me, managing to push concern and hilarity up into a glance. 'You wrote this down.'

'This?' I asked him, pointing up at the strange, narrowing boulevard, the curtain of high towers that even neglect had left behind. Wait a minute, this was *Steve's* building.

'I came over late last night, and we mapped out the day because you figured it might make it easier for me if we wrote everything down, where we'd go post-clinic, conversational gambits even. What was funny was your promise. You swore you wouldn't remember a word of it. But why don't you come up and see for yourself? I have your notes.'

'Okay,' I replied. What the hell else was I going to say? To imagine you could ever shrink the vagaries of life into book form was one kind of crazy, but to imagine life as a script, that was another bowl of Cheerios. Steve said not to worry, it was just the effects of the machine, and while readers might be confused at first, they would catch on quickly enough, just like I would. All too soon, he assured me, this opening to strange voices, to what we used to call love, would be happening all the time. His work, his machine, would ensure it.

When we got up to his apartment I looked over at a crumpled sheaf of legal paper adorned with my scrawl. I read, 'Auden, one day the humble scooter will make feet extinct!' and lay down on his fuchsia couch and sank into a deep and dreamless sleep. When I woke up, early the next morning, he was already gone.

Steve had great hopes for video when he began. He wanted to make videotapes that would be not only useful but fun. He loved reversible jackets, and sofas that turned into beds, and pens with compasses attached, so writers always knew what direction their stories were leaning into. He never had the easy money, never managed to climb up over the place that separated those who rolled around in cash all day from those who never had any, so it was important that his few possessions were multitaskers. He wanted to make a video you could eat after watching, with covers that inflated to become pillows or life preservers. He worked on a tape that was so strong you could tow a small car with it but that was also light and delicate enough to wrap a child's birthday present in. Video wasn't just for looking at anymore. It became, in Steve's hands, a Swiss army knife of the soul, its multiplex protrusions quickly unfolding to meet any emergency.

Steve never talked about it, but I knew that in secret he was trying to make a videotape that would cure AIDS. He felt that exposure to certain combinations of colour, in particular rhythms, could begin to remap the body's immune response. He'd drop by some mornings with his eyes staring dully at nothing at all, so I knew he'd been pressed up against the monitor all night, scoring the changes.

'I've decided,' he announced, and I watched with some fascination as a rare determination tried to root in that shapeless chin.

'What?' I finally asked him.

'The ugliest part of the body is someone's eyes.'

'Steve, how can you say that? I always fall in love with someone's eyes first and the rest of them follows.'

'It's no use protesting, I have proof.'

'What proof?'

'Every summer we draw closer to the sun by several thousand miles. The brighter, more direct light causes many to reach for their shades.'

'So?'

'Isn't it obvious? Even the dullest square on the block looks flash in Ray-Bans. Or take the censored pictures in the newspapers, the ones with the black line across the eyes. They're impossibly sexy because they're so mysterious.'

'But everyone looks a bit the same in Ray-Bans.'

'Exactly. Beauty is a shared ideal, and sunglasses are the expression of this ideal. I've started working on a video that will slowly darken the area around the eyes. Like a tanning machine for the face without the uv exposure.'

Steve liked to come by and talk shop. I know what he was trying to do. He was trying to get me out from underneath my body. Strangely enough, it usually worked, if only for a short time. He put on some new kind of cheer when he saw me, which was a little weird, because Steve's usually not cheery at all. He wasn't depressed or anything, but his happiness was a modest incline. When he greeted people, even friends he hadn't seen for years, he didn't kiss them, or throw his arms around familiar shoulders. Instead he drew them close and began to talk, wiping away the yesterdays with a steady run of nouns. There was a level calm he left behind, as if he were writing on water. I was grateful for this, though a little worried at the same time, because he didn't seem entirely himself. It was as if he had caught something coming here, or my apartment had become a fitting room for a new personality. This much was certain: he needed me, I knew that now. Or rather, his machine needed me. The machine that he claimed would one day appear like a book. He was the first to come under its influence and, for reasons I could hardly understand, the changes I saw growing up in front of me didn't fill me with apprehension, though it was clear enough by now that I would be next. I guess every machine we used, down to our can openers and nail clippers, all stowed their effects inside the body. Steve's invention would be no different, and while its promises seemed a long stretch of smaze, I found myself looking forward to them. One more thing I hadn't allowed myself for a long time. Anticipation.

In the past few months, after Steve's run with *The Lofters*, his number started showing up on corporate speed dials. There were boy bands looking for a video makeover, and then a local jeans outfit, and an infomercial for a bowling alley uptown. A cable channel was interested in something they called 'ambient television,' and there were regular meetings with a company hoping to renovate the light bulb. While he wasn't out pricing real-estate bling, Steve had enough small change to allow him to leave his office drudgeries behind. He would jog out of town on the weekend, sometimes as far as Europe or some new Japanese city looking for a facelift, presenting his video delicacies to the crush. But wherever he was headed, he made a point of stopping in first, sometimes making the airport cab wait while he underlined a point. He might bring along a tall boy of cider and a can of fish-oil caps. Selenium, vitamin B megatabs, whatever offered a glimmer. I shuffled out of bed whenever I could and said yes.

'I wish you could have met my friend Marcie before she died. I can't even show you a picture because she refused every kind of likeness. She had a special fibre woven into her cheeks that reflected light, so that even if you tried a surprise snap, her face would show up as a blank.'

I could tell by the way he trotted it out to me that he must have fought the urge himself. And in that moment it was possible to imagine Steve young again, though there was something in him that had always been old.

'I can't pull up her face, but I brought along this video to give you an idea of her work.'

In the past couple of visits he had hauled up a video player and a small colour TV set to replace the black-and-white I had filched from a dumpster. As we settled in to watch, I balanced a notepad on one knee and tried to get it all down without taking my eyes off the screen.

The video looked like it was shot from a seizure, everything appeared in multiple vantages, at once too close and too far. When I hit the pause button to ask, Steve admitted that he was wearing a camera jacket, an otherwise ordinary suit outfitted with small serial cameras. Which made me feel like I was inside his skin looking out, a not unpleasant sensation.

It was nighttime in what looked like Holland. Boats guided by gondoliers stole through dark canal waters, their only passengers small video projectors that shone up against buildings that lined the banks. What Steve was projecting onto the face of these old brickworks and new condos was the life inside: the morning pleasantries, the arguments and subtle dissuasions, the small hopes gathered beneath the name of family. Everyone came out to watch, and they looked startled by the revelation not of their neighbours but of themselves, appearing like the far shore of television. For this night at least, he had rendered the city transparent.

Now we were inside a cab speeding towards a public quorum in the city centre, the camera jacket offering competing vantages of a blurry picture-book downtown. The square was already filled with expectation and a DJ kept the untidy throngs on the edge of the cobblestones as Steve made his way to a large stage at the back of the square. I watched his hands twist an orange ribbon into the shapes of vowels, over and over again. After a brief introduction and the barest smattering of applause, he bent the microphone towards him and began to read from a nearly illegible text scribbled on the backs of five bar coasters. He had them lined up in a star, and passed his look easily from one to the next, as if he were knocking down drafts at the local.

'Marcie Zubareva was the only true genius I ever met,' Steve began. 'Unfortunately, her chosen vocation was video art, which ensured that no one but her closest friends would ever understand her. But even here, in a medium so obscure it makes poetry seem like the daily news, rumours of her talent began to circulate. Sneaker giants and cereal makers came to call, wondering at last if the grail of multinational capital was at hand. They hoped she might produce a picture that would fill each of its viewers with a perfect and individual happiness, and that this satisfaction would last only as long as its image and not a second more, creating in place of demand a necessity, a drive as fundamental as death itself.

'Little did they realize that she had arrived at just such an image early in her work, only to find that the emotion each of her viewers longed for was not happiness at all, but an escape from feelings of every kind, a numbing paralysis that allowed each of us – and I have to include myself here, because I was one of the few to see it – to feel comfortable with one another. No, it was more than that. Her work allowed us to experience the subatomic unions that lay all around our inert and unfeeling bodies. I'm not ashamed to say that I soon became a regular visitor to her cramped basement apartment, offering to clean dishes or wipe the floor or anything, really, in the hope that I might see, just one more time, the motion picture she had made so quickly, and then decided, after a screening in the local diner, to set aside forever.

'Finally, she conceived of a tape that would summarize not just her own life but the history of everyone she had ever met, and owing to her extreme modesty, she aimed to use just a single frame of video. Her last eight years were consumed with this task. In the first four years she built a monumental video, 1,000 hours long, which embraced every aspect of human expression. In the next four years she condensed her project, offering a dizzying series of layered pictures, which appeared like an archaeology of mind. Determined to achieve clarity and a simplicity of design, she drove herself relentlessly, working night and day, until she arrived at a solution that was radically simple. Excited, feverish, she completed her masterwork on her birthday, and then passed into a coma from which she would never recover. She had just turned forty-three.

'But she had finished her project, though it would divide critics in the years following her death. Some read her surviving masterpiece as a secret history of the body. Others maintained that an occult design clung to it, and there were rumours that sects had formed to worship it in private. Finally, everyone could agree only that it was equal parts memorial and celebration, a letter from beyond the grave to those left behind. It was certainly the shortest video ever made, consisting of just a single frame that dared to contain all images and sounds ever produced.

'Worried that this artifact of marginal culture might inspire panic in the general public, its release was initially withheld. It has been kept in a special vault in the National Archives until now, when it can finally be shown without fear of censorship or reprisals. Like all forward-looking art, it requires a special kind of attention, an audience as wise and fully formed as the work itself. I hope you enjoy it.'

And with that, Steve stepped into the night that lay beyond the dais, and hurried off, and when I looked up to ask him if he had helped her with the project I was startled to find that he had already left. I scanned the tape again, looking for evidence of this wondrous video, this single frame of zeitgeist that I imagined working like orange concentrate, but I couldn't find anything. The tape ended in a burst of white-noise static, so I wrote that down too.

The work of the machine went on and I was glad to follow, slowly gathering pages that seemed strangely independent of the events they described. When I looked them over they spoke to me in a voice, Steve's voice, that I recognized increasingly as my own. Somehow the words of the machine enacted a steady incoming tide, the gentlest kind of pressure exerted itself, slowly wearing away thoughts that used to sound in my own voice. Steve said that the voice I used to have was 'like a face drawn in the sand at the edge of the sea,' a phrase he insistently borrowed from someone else. Soon we would recognize that all of our phrases belonged to someone else. *Hi, how are you? It's nice to meet you. I love you.* All I knew for certain was that the voice I heard increasingly, inside and out, seemed to belong to Steve. Its soft reliable tones made even angry words desirable. I was learning. Becoming part of the machine.

I tried not to hate them. The normals. The ones who treated illness as a temporary disturbance, a speed bump on the way to their leisure machines. I tried not to think of how I could bleed into the city's water supply and take them all down with me. I tried not to blame everyone who was not already infected, but it was hard. The papers were filled with columns about positive men arrested for having unprotected sex. Pregnant mothers pointed outraged fingers as the most private of exchanges turned up on police blotters. While I was horrified by these predatory behaviours, I understood the impulse. The message they were trying to write in their monster's blood was simple: *We're all in this together.*

I finally made my way back to the doctor who smelled like sugar and picked up the script he had waiting on file. When I arrived, he brandished it like a matador's cape and handed it right over before even saying hello. Perhaps there wasn't time for hello anymore. I smiled when he said, like he always said, in his best James Brown imitation, 'It's for your own good thing.' The waiting room was filled with thinning men young and old, many with canes propped up beside them, trying to lose themselves in the latest gardening glossies or sporting updates. The secretary called everyone by some shortened version of their first name in order to promote – as he made a point of telling all the new clients – a 'relaxed' and 'informal' atmosphere. But he held up with me because no matter how he cut it, *Auden* only short-formed into *Odd*, and that sounded a bit too informal.

I filled the script downstairs and came home with a large paper bag filled with childproof bottles. Newspapers dubbed it the 'cocktail,' though there were so many pills, all requiring different moments of ingestion, that the cocktail hour never really ended. Why did I find it so difficult to be grateful? I under-stood that the new meds would run me down a little further before the promised salvation occurred, but the doc promised that soon enough whole days might be spent outside in the shade. Feeling again. For the past weeks feeling had been just pain, and fevers and nausea, and organs in revolt, so I tried to keep it down to a minimum. But soon, how soon, each day might be proof that feeling could be admitted without punishment. A new world was beginning, which looked much like the old one, except now there were a few dazed pill-heads like myself, young and just past death. More determined than ever to release a plague upon this earth. A plague of normal.

I rang Johnson and told him that the mysterious debilities that had been turning me into a full-time bed tester had finally been diagnosed: I had Lyme disease. I don't think he bought it for a moment, but we both felt reassured that at last we had a name to throw around.

'Lyme disease, it sounds green,' he said as if he were reading a traffic report.

'Different kind of lime, Johnson. This one comes with ticks.'

'Like a hot dog and mustard.'

'Something like that.'

He wasn't on the hook for paying me while I was away on leave, so there was a natural curb to his dissatisfactions. I would be back, I assured him, though not just yet. He grunted through my explanations, then filled my ears with the story of a family-run convenience store robbed by the owner's son in a hockey mask. His own father had gunned him down at the cash before police took the hood off, and now the family stood on a fat life insurance claim. Was it fair? Johnson couldn't have sounded more hurt if he had lost his own son.

'This is really the thin end, Auden. What are we going to do? The payout is so big, we might not even be able to keep Cary on. Our insurers are talking to their insurers, you know what I mean?'

'I know what you mean,' I told him.

'Even if the old man gets put away, the policy says they still collect. Listen, don't ever get involved with families. Mothers, brothers, never mind. It's a whatchamacallit, a conspiracy. A blood conspiracy, that's what it is. There should be laws to protect us against this.'

He told me to hold up a minute and started chatting with Cary, and then another voice I didn't recognize, and after a few minutes of this I started coughing and asking, 'Johnson? Johnson?' Over and over. And even when he said, 'Yes, yes,' I kept right on asking as if I couldn't hear a word he said. And then I hung up.

When I pulled up to Steve's apartment, I saw there was a five-star production in progress, big lozenges of trailer lined up and down the block. I strolled past and, sure enough, his face pinned to the set, there was Steve. I walked over and gave his arm a little squeeze, just to let him know I was around, but he had eyes only for his very own corner store and laundromat, now converted into backdrops for stars. Was that Joan Collins standing beside the lotto adverts? Wearing a sassy power suit and enough shiny rock to fund a small revolution. She was getting some hair patted back into place, bigging up the stairclimber do that launched her second career, was it, or her third? She looked shorter than I had imagined, except for the head, which sat like a hot-air balloon on those shoulder pads, threatening to lift off on its own every time she opened that million-dollar mouth. She didn't seem especially happy and was letting everyone know, especially some short guy with a backasswards Yankees cap covering the inevitable bald patch. He had to be the director. He was twenty-five going on ninety, some little brat-packer whose idea of a good time was memorizing the shot list from *Mean Streets*. He'd rather be back in the studio letting the 3-D boys put the action figures through their paces. But no, he was stuck out here in reptile weather, trying to get old Joan up for one more take.

Steve pulled me closer and we huddled together in the small tangle of onlookers, fascinated by the slow-motion production mechanics. 'Don't let the setting fool you,' he advised. 'This movie is a romance, otherwise Joan wouldn't be involved.' But as the grips and electricals stood listless in an overheated frieze, it was clear that this love story was being made without any love at all. It was exactly this disconnect that kept Steve roosting in the scrum. He was convinced it couldn't work, but had to see whether Joan could reach through all that corporate gloss and deliver.

The scene looked pretty simple. Joan was supposed to do a blab and grab at the jewellery counter, and when the cashier catches up with her on the sidewalk she begs him to forget today ever happened. In fact, the way the director kept pointing down at the pavement I think she was supposed to get down and do some serious whimpering, but something about the way she had her arms folded across her chest said no, she just couldn't. Crushed wasn't part of her play card. She'd been fighting the better part of the last century to drop that gear, so go ahead, ask her to do almost anything, just don't try getting her to roll over and say please. Disgusted, Joan snapped at the woman doing her hair, and the mouse dutifully combed the long black curls up, up and away. Joan paused, lit a cigarette and then announced loudly enough for us to hear it clear across the street, 'There are no small movies. Only small directors.'

Even though there were mornings when I could hardly leave my swimming pool of a bed and rub two thoughts together, Steve kept dropping by, and each time he did we took up the work of 'building the machine,' as he called it, which made me feel a bit like I was back at school, taking dictation from a particularly lucent professor of digression. This writing machine wasn't going to launch anyone into orbit, or inoculate the swelling global underclass against illnesses that had been 'cured' decades ago, but it was a reason to get up each morning, and for that I was grateful.

Steve led us outside to the upscale doughnut shop perched conveniently around the corner. Last month it was the smell of bacon, this month the thought of pigs frying made him weak. When I suggested another spot, he shifted in his seat, looking like someone had let a bag of fire ants loose in his underthings. 'It never closes here,' he said, as if the promise of an infinite doughnut were enough. And some mornings it was. I had taken to writing on napkins while we talked, they were cheap and in good supply here, and because I usually averaged at least a honey cruller, a glazed something and an apple fritter every thirty minutes, my mind was so numbed with sugar that I found it hard to remember anything. It was a good thing the napkins were able to soak up the afternoon or it would all drift away.

Steve always wanted to talk to me about art, which was funny, because it wasn't something that ever ran on the news, or in magazines. I guess all the really famous artists were already dead, so putting them on covers would only be depressing. But Steve insisted that one day *People* magazine would be empty because we wouldn't be caring about people anymore. Art, he insisted, was preparing us for a time when humans were no longer at the centre of things. 'And in our place?' I asked him, but he only looked back with a smile and a half across his mug, like he knew the score but he couldn't let on or the ghosts of past inventors might strike him dumb.

As I continued to write, I noticed how every napkin was made of softspun squares, small paper diamonds each a little different than its neighbour. Inside these micro-worlds I could see the two of us talking, thousands of us copied and copied again, the smallest moment of some global DNA ... and then everything went black and there was nothing. Nothing at all.

When I came around, Steve was still laughing. He couldn't believe it, he said. It wasn't every day a face plant that perfect landed in the centre of a strawberry jelly doughnut. With a delicacy he must have stowed for special occasions like this one, he daubed away the sugary remains from my face and eased me back into the chair before we set off. I didn't notice everyone staring at us until we got to the door, like we were on television or something, and as I considered making an exit bow, Steve urged me outside and slowly down the heaving concrete.

'The way their bodies become a way to look at you, doesn't it ever untie your bow?' I asked, but he said no, not at all. He had grown up in an apartment building, the world was his neighbour, and who cared what the neighbours thought? Which didn't entirely excuse his wardrobe. His sweater boasted orange lightning bolts streaking across what looked like a background of tomato vomit, which pushed even Steve's notorious absence of taste into unexplored territory. Incredible to think they could manufacture colours that ugly, certain that someone would find in them a finer, more virtuous version of himself. It was Steve's idea of beautiful, and the terrifying thing was that he might not be alone.

At last we arrived at Steve's anonymous door, identical in every respect to the dozens of others that lined these halls. I felt them decomposing into dark tears that pooled across the walls and ran in little eddies beneath our feet, until Steve grabbed hold of me and pushed me through the entrance. The room swelled up with every breath and then shrank down to the size of a shot-glass until Steve performed a welcome distraction. Swaying once, he lifted his unseemly frame into a posture that lay somewhere between a Russian gymnast on downers and a Hanna-Barbera creation taking a particularly nasty pratfall. I slumped into the nearest chair, grateful to be inside four walls again, and looked down into Steve's notebook, lying open at today's date, and found everything already written there. The doughnut store whiteout, the search for keys and an ensuing conversation that was less amusing than enigmatic. The lines swam into focus. Why did he bother to write this stuff down, I wondered, as I read the words 'Steve looked into me … '

Steve looked into me, wondering if I had understood. Personality was only an imperfect collection of memories, and now that art had set itself the task of leaving personality behind, we would pass in and out of one another like so many interchangeable parts. Like a machine. I wrote that down too, trying to resist the urge to look across the table and see it already waiting in black and white, staring back from the pages of Steve's journal.

When I glanced up again, I realized that he had left without a sound. I called his name into the empty rooms but there was no reply, and I wondered how long I had been sitting there alone, while Steve stage-managed his entrances and exits, dissolving back into the words he was sure would be the only thing he would leave behind.

Steve was already inside the crowded waiting room of the clinic when I arrived, its perfect couches filled with grrrls in plastic pants chafed with excitement. They were at the age when events of any kind were greeted with the same high-pitched squeal. Even catastrophe seemed to delight them. Steve looked a little worn this afternoon, like he'd been rubbing his face up against a wedge of sandpaper. It had been strange not seeing him for the past couple of days, though there was still his voice, of course, always running in my head, so it was as if he never really left. Whenever I heard him up close and personal I couldn't help feel a little startled pop go off, like some bit of my intestines had been left to wander alone in the world, freed from the tyranny of the body. He slid over beside me and leaned in close.

'When I rang up earlier, the hireling answered everything on the short side. "Yes. Can. I. Help. You?" But when I offered my name he said, "Yes, Mr. Armstrong." Without skipping a beat, like he'd had the chart up in front of him all day.'

Steve had tested under the name Neil Armstrong as a nod to his fave astronaut. The clinic encouraged aliases and I wondered how many had chosen Armstrong before him.

'And then there's this pause, and I think the line's gone dead, and I'm just about to say grace before he comes back on and says, "Your. Tests. Are. In." Like he knew something he shouldn't know.

I told him it was nothing, reception was likely caught up in some paperclip rebellion, maybe a couple of files collided, who knows. But the heaviness was real. Everyone here had made the same call, waiting to find out from the oracles of science whether they still had a future. For my part, I felt superstition take hold. I tried crossing my legs and then opening them, concentrating on a healing number. What was a healing number? Is seven for

good health or good luck, or was there really any difference now?
I worried the disease would find Steve through me, maybe
because my hair was parted the wrong way, or because I was
thinking of the wrong goddamn healing number, so even though
he was fine walking in here, he was probably getting storm troop-
ered by infection right now, leaned up against the condom racks
and warning pamphlets.

At last the young doctor reappeared with a face that already
seemed a mask of apology. His white coat and clipboard served
notice that the inferno was a science, not an art, that the unthinkable had become ordinary. Patience, his face counselled, this was
not the last place. This was where you came before the end. There
would be many stops along the way.

He called out for a lanky skateboarder already balding at
twenty-five, maybe from the home bleach job that had turned the
remains of his hair a worried shade of green. Mr. Skateboard
floated across the room like a warning beacon and disappeared
down the hallway. Another door opened for one of the giggle
twins while her better half immediately composed herself, reaching into her purse for a round of blush. On the last day of the
world, she would be ready for her close-up.

'I think I know that guy,' Steve said to me as he pointed at the
closed door with his nose.

'What guy?'

'The one with the green hair. He's a regular at Armitage
Shanks. Or at least his living mirror look-alike is a regular. The
whole place probably meets here after closing.'

'Could two people really have the same bad idea about colour-
ing what's left of their hair?' I asked him, not really expecting
an answer.

'Oh sure, just think of Elvis,' he said without elaborating, throwing a battered copy of *Wired* back on the table. He wasn't angry exactly, but resigned. Tired. I felt a sudden longing to become the winged sprite that opened each title sequence of *The Wonderful World of Disney*. I wanted to hover for a moment in the blind spot of everyone gathered here and whisper into their ears, 'You are beautiful and deserving of love.' I would repeat this greeting-card mantra until it took root and enveloped each of them in a wash of brilliant light, saving the chartreuse for Steve because it was his favourite. Then I would glide out the window in search of every lonely bus-stop-waiting, solitary-doughnut-store-eating, afraid-to-leave-their-apartment shutaway that I could find and offer them the same assurance. I would make a living by offering extended sessions to a select clientele, for instance, ex–TV game show hosts, or anyone who had suffered overnight success, or who had never had their heart broken. Of course, I didn't do any of this. I stared at my hands and the worn-down nubs of the wall-to-wall carpeting, feeling that every word I ever knew was something strange and far away.

'Nobody voted for those,' Steve told me, waving his hand towards reception.

'Say what?' I asked.

'Nobody voted for computers. Or atom bombs.'

Or AIDS, I wanted to say, finishing the sentence, but stopped myself. While there were posters and pamphlets screaming 'AIDS' from every wall, no one here spoke the word. Its pronouncement was reserved for the other place, where professionals exchanged with their anonymous clientele the secrets of their own naming.

'In a real democracy, the democracy of the future, we'll be able to vote for our parents, and all the diseases we can expect in our lifetime will be made available in a multiple-choice quiz with minimum selection requirements.' Steve announced this to me with the finality of a newscaster. The future had become a second home for him, while the present remained a painful reminder of how far we still had to go.

'So certain kinds of sick would vanish because no one chooses them?' I offered.

'Like bowler hats or bow ties. They'd go out of fashion,' Steve insisted.

'I can imagine the advertising already. Runway shows for the common cold.'

'Think of it.'

'I'm trying.'

The girl-woman, the one who turned to her friends and announced, 'I'm going to turn a hundred in this dress, just like my grandmother!' before she left, reappeared with all of her eyeliner run down the left side of her face. I knew it was harsh but I couldn't help thinking it might not be AIDS, it could be herpes or syphilis or pregnancy. People still got pregnant, didn't they? Knowing that was small consolation now. Her friend was up in a shot and took her arm like she'd become old all of a sudden. They headed towards the exit, squeezing past the folks who continued to appear from the stairwell, as if from a roll call of the damned. Everyone tried not to look but we couldn't help it, all of us hoped that perhaps for today this sacrifice would be enough, comestibles for the gods who presided over the body of the world, knitting together the beginning and the end. As they hit the door, her friend looked back to where they'd sat, minutes before, laughing as if the nineteen summers they'd enjoyed were the smallest moment of an infinite horizon, that they could scatter time as they skipped across the globe like tycoons of chronology, reckless.

'Mr. Armstrong?'

'Yes,' Steve said, rising from the couch.

I gave Steve's shoulder a squeeze as he lifted away from the wall, only he wasn't feeling it, his eyes were fixed on the doctor's manila folder. I picked up the copy of *Wired* that Steve had dropped on the table, hoping to escape into geektopia. The layout was so thick I could hardly make out a word, though I found the obscurity somehow reassuring. In *Wired*'s brave new netspeak, meaning resided not in the eye's travel over miles of text, but in a sudden gestalt, where layers of corporate gloss resolved in a sudden and unexpected focus. Do you speak computer? The green-haired man reappeared and the crowd around the door parted to let him through, though he hardly seemed to notice. He didn't care any longer; he was one of the lucky ones, able to leave as if this afternoon had never made its way onto the calendar. He had run the gauntlet of this illness with the same what-me-worry? step and emerged untouched, ready to be reclaimed by the world of the healthy.

The longer Steve was on the other side, swallowed up by the bad fluorescent lighting and the grime-battered blinds that gave the office a sense of perpetual dusk, the worse it felt. How much time did it take for someone to say yes or no? I cheered myself with the thought that the two of them could be smiling into each other's arms, while some part of Steve's overly large brain batch-digitized the whole experience for use in his next video. But as the waiting room slowly cleared, another conclusion began to assert itself. The only reason he was still in there had to be ... No, I just couldn't think about that, not here, when there was nothing else to think. What was going on in there?

The clinic had grown quiet, the waiting room emptied into the small doors that waited beyond the desk, where the fortune tellers of medicine pronounced destinies written in blood. All day long and well into the night the clinic received visitors, though for each it was an encounter they would not soon forget. It was difficult, perhaps impossible, not to feel it also as a kind of judgment, especially for the unlucky ones. They were the first to ask: Why me? What did I do?

Steve finally appeared from the looming doors, and I couldn't tell from his face whether this was the first day of his life or the last. He motioned to me from the other side of the desk, past the audience of the doomed, and as soon as we hit pavement he laid down a fart that sounded like a chainsaw starting up. I couldn't help laughing, only I didn't know if I was allowed, if that was the worst thing I could do now. Or whether the worst had already happened. I put my arm around him as we turned the corner towards the underground.

'So, what's the story?' I asked him, trying for casual. We chumped down the stairs centimetres away from a Filipino man so wide I don't know how he made it through the turnstile. He carried a large wooden bat that hovered perilously close to my face as Steve ventured a reply.

'The doctor looked down my file for a long second and said, "Mr. Armstrong, I don't want to keep you waiting any longer," and I urged him to take as much time as he needed. I assured him that I loved to wait. Waiting to get into something is always more exciting than seeing it.'

He smiled at me, or tried to. The lips opened to reveal years of indifferent dental care. It was as if half his face were smiling while the other half asked: Are you kidding? Smile, at a time like this?

'He said, "I'm afraid you've got it. They'll do another test to verify ... "'

He never finished the sentence. We took the eastbound train because that was the one that came first and got off a few stops later. We jogged up the moving stairs, going nowhere in particular at top speed. Every time we hit a light we'd bounce right off and head in whatever direction lay open to us, just so long as we could keep momentum. Finally we found ourselves in an area of town neither of us had seen except on maps. We were dead hungry, but Steve didn't trust himself inside yet, not even here, surrounded by strangers. I was starting to wobble in the glare, pulled along in the wake of his irresistible rush towards the unknown, which relented at last in a small pizza joint that had refused global replication. I tried to bring back the lines I'd been rehearsing the past week, but the comfort-inducing syntax seemed too small to fit. We held hands beneath the disapproving glance of the kid behind the ovens, who figured we must be saying goodbye or something, wondering why we'd ever come to a crummy little place like this to break off the affair.

'Twenty-five heads of the Klan lived past eighty, more than fifteen years past the median age in their districts. They had fine southern funerals with sympathy dish gardens and men in handsome suits offering eulogies.'

'Is that what you want?'

'I'm in a pizza house and I don't even like pizza. I don't know what I want.'

He rubbed at the small place between his eyes, speaking to himself, to me, the oversized hot-sauce bottles waiting on the table. He didn't seem particularly upset, not yet, only determined, as if it were a matter now of lifting his game, pushing a little harder in order to get through every goddamn day after day. I wanted to give him one more hour of not knowing. I wanted to roll back the tape until we were back at the street corner a thousand years ago, deciding to forget all about the clinic.

'Being positive isn't ... ' I started.

'I know that.'

' ... the end.'

He turned to me then, looking more confused than I'd ever seen him. He had landed in the foreign capital of his own life.

'I just can't see why anyone would ever, whether I would have taken the risk if I knew before we ... '

'Touched?' I asked him.

'Touched, yes, that I could actually go through with it. What sort of person is worth that kind of risk?' He squinted through the trouble eating at his face.

'I did. You did,' I assured him.

'But we didn't know,' Steve insisted.

'Would that have really stopped us?'

'From love, you mean?'

'From love.'

Tears fell on the bright yellow Formica, pooling up against the disinfectant spray and industrial-strength cleaners. He was so broken, so hurt, *so human*, I thought to myself. For a moment I almost preferred it. I caught the voice inside me declaring, 'I like you when you're like this. I could love you if you were like this. Shattered. Like the rest of us.'

'To find someone who is positive, to pick them out of a crowd and say *you*. Not that one or that one, I want *you*. How could I ever want to be with someone who would do a thing like that? Some loser already halfway off the ledge,' he said, the sadness already turning into something like angry.

'Steve, I want you to do something for me. When lunch arrives, I want you to chew down each bite as slow as you can. Just get hold of every fucking bite and chew it real slow, you got that?'

'I'm sorry.'

'For what? Testing positive?'

'For not being careful. For looking at the end and saying okay. Or at least maybe. Maybe I will. Maybe I won't.'

'Will you ease up on that for a minute? It's not about blame.'

'The well-rehearsed words.'

'It's not your fault.'

'Repeated over and over.'

'And it's not the end.'

'And when the last door closes, it's time to begin again. Look, ladies and gentlemen, you haven't seen this one yet. We call it hope.'

The pizza arrived and we refuelled, jacking the burnt peppers and anchovies directly into the cerebral cortex where they could manufacture new words for loss. Pizzabilities: that's what the sign on the door read. The counter held up a hardbody in a crew-cut, his large hands folding a double slice into equal triangles before swallowing. His T-shirt read *I am a convicted shoplifter*, and the bright orange letters were hard to miss. 'This way I always get the best service. Never have to wait for nothing.' The words hung there in the space between us, flat and even with the dullness that healthy people bring to everything. His voice, long ago tired of listening to itself, announced that it was just another afternoon, another pizza with double ham hold the pineapple, another stranger in a bad T-shirt with time on his side. Everything belonged here except for us.

'After the good doctor told me, I started to wonder whether there hadn't been some kind of mistake. He was reading off a column of figures that were all that really separated me from what I used to be. So without asking, because it's my life, right, I reach over and pull the file to my side of the table. Sure enough, there's a little red box with a cross through it and the word *seropositive* right beside that. And then the name: Neil Armstrong. For a second – was it longer than that? – I felt free, like this was all a big mistake. I could go home now knowing everything's all right because I wasn't positive after all, it's Neil. It's been Neil the whole time.'

'Yes, but ... '

'And then I realized I picked him. Picked Neil out of the crowd. And Neil's always been positive. So the moment I decided ... '

'You decided.'

He slumped back from the table, a straggly bit of cheese substitute clinging to his chin, robbing him of whatever dignity he hadn't already left at the clinic. He shook his head no. Like he wanted to take today off the calendar. I wanted to touch him, hold him, but he looked so far away I wasn't sure I'd make up the distance. Coward to the end.

'Steve, you remember the story you told me about how things weren't working out with that football genius you dated – David?'

'It was so cold that winter, five degrees below the mean. David would get cold just looking at pictures of snow, and every year when winter hit ... '

'You found a beach, a little spot just outside of ... '

'Daytona.'

'Daytona, yes. And when you came back, David had that ridiculous sun hat he wouldn't take off. You kept telling him that he only had to hit that beach one time because it would always be there for him. Hot and perfect with the clear waves rolling out. Anytime he wanted he could always go back, no matter how cold it was. It wasn't a vacation or a break from his life, but it was more real than anything around him.'

'So what you're saying is ... '

'I think it's time to go to the beach.'

We started the long trudge back, pretending we were on boogie boards riding a mile-high curl back into downtown, but after a few blocks gravity returned us to the present. It had been a long day.

The next morning I came by for a visit, the worry running between my shoulders. No matter how many times I unpacked my face and put it back together again, the bad feeling stepped right through it. I wanted to rub his tired feet, or distract him with malignant gossip, or do any damned useful thing, knowing this category of action had been reserved for professionals. Which meant only that I arrived looking far worse than Steve, though he pretended not to notice, regaling me instead with thoughts on his new wardrobe. He was lounging in an all-white paper suit he had picked up from the hardware store for three dollars. He was so thrilled at the price he bought a dozen and swore he wouldn't wear anything else. Ever.

'It's so I can remember,' he said. 'Whenever I want to scare up this time again I'll just have to think, "White suit," and it will all come rushing back.'

'You just turned positive and you're worried about whether you're going to remember everything or not?'

'It's a new period in my life. It wants a new look.'

I imagined teams of crack scientists parachuted into viral jungles, suited up against the plague. They would look just like this. But nothing I could say would dissuade, so I let it slip. And after a few days the suits began to lose their shine, so he didn't look so much like a bright blazing pad of paper moving through the world. Just a little rumpled, that's all. It was hard to iron paper.

The apartment, Steve's apartment, had never looked quite so full. He'd given up doing anything that didn't promise pleasure or reward, so there were stacks of dishes over everything, discarded magazines and a milk carton, left standing from a sudden urge for protein last week, which was slowly turning into whatever milk became when it tired of itself. Opening the door to let me in, Steve pushed aside heaps of CDs and a pocket-size box of dog vittles (what *does* dog food taste like?), and I cramped up with worry because I'd never seen his place look anything but crisp and ready for inspection. He told me that he was determined to fill his apartment up, like a sweet gin martini. He wanted to live vertically, having grown tired of spreading out in the other direction, across land.

'So what happens when your apartment is full, like – what did you say?'

'Like a sweet gin martini.'

'So what happens then?'

'Then I'll drink it all down and start over.'

I don't think I'd ever seen him happier. He looked relaxed and boneless, ready to slide into whatever remained of his life. He had installed a private karaoke unit, one of those hundred-dollar knock-offs making the infomercial rounds, and was busy nights learning the words to a scatter of new Japanese pop hits.

')*(%^%$$$GDG_(***,' he crooned to me in a language I couldn't help feeling bore only a vague resemblance to its Japanese original.

'What's that?'

'It means: my heart is full and my brain is empty. I'm in love with you you you.'

'If they dropped the bomb and all that was left was a karaoke machine, do you think you could reconstruct a culture from that?'

'Are you kidding? Life as a musical. What could be sweeter?'

Even his laugh had changed. He always had a sense of humour, of course. But there was something a little forced about his pre-clinic laughter. Full-throttled amusement might occasion a reluctant lifting of shoulders while his head bobbed, as if he were pushing something out of himself, birthing an amused chortle or an ironic snicker. His laugh belonged to the fifties, or at least fifties television, when the emotional range of characters was deliberately suppressed. Television was a new medium then, and no one knew what unleashing a torrent of feeling into the nation's living rooms might provoke. It was an early version of Prozac Nation featuring a stunned procession of small-town cheer, and as long as I'd known him, Steve had acted like he'd just walked off the set of one of those programs. Today, his roundness was gone, replaced with something almost animal, as if his laugh had grown teeth. So I had to ask him.

'Steve?'

'Yeah.'

'You know the experiment you were conducting with dog food?'

'The one that asked whether dog food had supplements that made dogs more loyal and obedient, while cat food had additives that ensured they would be more independent and cute.'

'Yeah.'

'What about it?'

'How long did your new diet last?'

'A week of each, more or less. I took vitamin supplements, of course, and occasionally begged scraps from the dinner tables of friends. But because I could control the food source, the results were … '

'Suboptimal?'

'Preliminary. I wound up behaving like any other good doggie and stuffed myself without restraint. I must have put on ten pounds.'

'And you didn't notice any other changes?'

'I never had the urge to pee on fire hydrants, if that's what you mean.'

'Never mind. Never mind.'

'What?'

'You just seem ... different somehow.'

'Bad different?'

'Too early to tell.'

'What you're responding to is just PTS: Personality Template Shift. I go through one every seven or eight years. Auden, our personalities are only temporary, a fact that few of us have bothered to learn. They were never designed for the long haul. They're too fragile and subject to breaking down. Imagine driving the same car all your life, wearing the same pair of pants, using the same toothbrush. Sooner or later, they're going to stop working.'

'So every once in a while ... '

'Myself, I prefer the lives of people in books. They're a little deeper, a little richer somehow than anyone you actually meet, don't you think?'

'Steve, this is all sounding very ... '

'Look, most people just take what comes along. They're gene slaves. They toe a line in the sand next to Mom and Dad and never really budge. The rest of their life is just accessorizing. Fussing out the details. Maybe a new wardrobe, new job, new lover. But what if you let go? What if personality wasn't fixed after all but more like shopping?'

'What if?' I asked him.

'Take you, for instance,' Steve continued. 'You rarely start conversations, you respond. You pick your spots and chime in.

Which means that mostly you have to listen while others talk. This suits you pretty well because being a listener makes you appear sensitive. But secretly you hate listening. You're only really comfortable when you can be alone because of the talking that's always going on inside your head. You can only hear one voice at a time, and because the one inside never stops telling you what you should be doing, or how you should be feeling, there isn't room for much else. The truth is, Auden, you don't really have a personality. You have this voice, and you follow it everywhere.'

I got up to pour us another round of crantinis, though when I searched for the small daisy-coloured umbrellas he enjoyed turning to make a point, I found the drawer stuffed to bursting with blurred playing cards.

'Like a reader, you mean,' I asked him.

'Yes.'

'You mean I hear a voice inside my head the way a reader hears a voice whenever they're moving through a book.'

'That's it exactly.'

'Only the book never stops, is that it?'

'The book is part of a machine. And you are also part of that machine. You've devoted your life to adding parts to this machine, so that others will join you there and become infected by this voice. You think somehow that if other people heard this voice, it would ease your burden. The burden of having to listen to it all the time.'

'Is that what love is? Infecting people with the voice?'

'No, that's what reading is. Love, on the other hand, is about ... '

The phone rang and he jumped to answer it. A major cable network was sinking into a ratings mire despite raves from its in-house focus groups. Now it wanted to run out-of-focus groups and was hoping that Steve could help it reorganize. He had been conducting focus experiments with some success lately and word had spread quickly. He smiled into the receiver for a long while, pausing now and then to say 'Yes' and 'Sure' and 'Certainly yes.' I looked down at the words on the page, the afternoon's tidy pile accumulating on the table. And wondered at the voice held inside those lines like a promise, waiting for unmet readers to set it into motion. Like a car and its driver. It was difficult to imagine that they would collect inside its readers and slowly form a new voice there, but because it was already happening to me, I could hardly doubt it. I looked over to where Steve had turned himself round and round the phone cord like an electric version of King Tut. He caught my eye and threw both hands in the air, then stared helplessly back at the phone, intoning, 'Yes. Yes. Yes.'

We set off to an underground soirée hosted in a suitably dingy corner of the city. Yoko Ono was rumoured to be there, so Steve was pretty pumped. As a boy, he had loved her singing; her shrill, penetrating shriek had never failed to comfort him. Inspired by her efforts, he began to ring out the many singsongs that filled his daydreams; indeed, everything around him appeared as music, from the aimless chatter of adults to the hum of refrigerators. Soon, he lived for the moments when he could belt out tunes improvised around electro-clash themes, and as a young boy he took every opportunity to share his gift: in line-ups at the SuperSave, meetings of the Thornhill Women's Bowling League or wherever his poor mother would take him. The songs were rung out at full volume and lay invariably flat, though the music Steve heard within was a rapturous melody. It wasn't until his mother had the bright idea of recording the boy, cajoling him to listen to the sound of his own voice, that he stopped, fascinated and repelled by the strangled notes that issued from the cheap recorder.

For years he sang nothing further, until he heard, on a late-night station, the shrieks of Yoko Ono sounding so much like his own. He fell instantly in love with that voice. Like most teenagers, he kept busy falling in love with parts of people: Joni Mitchell's hands, for instance, or the way Elton John's chest hair grew straight up into his face. With Yoko it was her voice. He understood instinctively that she had conquered the fear of bad taste and impropriety that stopped almost everyone from feeling pleasure.

That night he looked forward to meeting her for the first time, and he asked me along, naturally presuming that I would be equally thrilled to welcome the Fluxus godmother. From the time we entered the door to the time we left, Steve never said a word, even after he was introduced to Yoko, who looked pretty swank in her dark beret and tinted glasses. After an overly long and particularly awkward introduction, Steve opened his mouth, but no sound came out. With the kindness that only a veteran junket queen could muster, Yoko flashed him a winning smile, and then we were on our way.

'What was that all about?' I asked, and he shrugged, saying that he'd pulled out some of her old records and began practicing scales outside the frequency range of most listeners. When she smiled, he knew that she had heard him and understood. He had made his ugliness invisible, except for those who shared the gift.

Steve had already begun work on what was to become *The Hundred Videos* when we met. It occupied him the way an invading army occupied a new country, and when it was done everyone wanted a piece. There was the strange appearance on *Letterman* where he entertained the studio audience by showing them videos that allowed them to see five seconds into the future, causing them to howl and applaud before the punchlines hit. The following night, when fellow guest Julia Roberts walked on the *Leno* set, he deadpanned, 'You're beautiful enough for the three of us.' Everyone laughed except Leno because Steve had plucked it right off the teleprompter. There were magazine covers where he allowed photographers only the back of his head. Radio interviews where he would answer either yes or no, prompting either desperate silence or increasingly fantastical responses from his hosts. Bar coasters would disappear between sips, neighbours who had made a point of pretending he never existed cozied up to him, his Visa slips were preserved for the sanctity of his autograph.

During his fifteen minutes of celebrity poses, Steve maintained a resigned stoicism, more comfortable behind the camera than in front of it. He persevered nonetheless, and when I asked him why he bothered he slumped deeper into one of the muddied white suits he wore no matter what the season. Steve assured me he didn't know why. And it was funny because he didn't sound like himself when he said it. Only it wasn't the voice. The voice was right there, smooth and flat and imperturbable. But the words he used didn't sound like Steve at all. I clocked him then and kept an ear out for it, and, sure enough, in the days ahead, he seemed to change with the weather. The voice covered it up mostly, but it was as if he didn't really have a personality, only different modes of presentation. He always sounded like someone else, and I wondered why I had never caught this before.

I guessed that he must have been feeling the effects of one of his machines. He had built videotape machines in the past that had allowed his lovers to become more perfect versions of themselves. But what we had been building together involved a more fundamental rewiring. He was blowing open the doors of personality and allowing the language of others to inhabit him. Like a virus.

But in those bright and temporary weeks of Steve-mania, none of that mattered either. He had become a picture of himself, so despite his recent diagnosis, he was fabulously sexy for those who knew him least of all. He didn't have to bother with introductions, the comfort of strangers relied on the magnetic charm that passed through him. He was always careful to wear protection, of course, there would be no sharing of an affliction that had already been broadly publicized. He was quietly surprised at how easy safer sex was after all, and how much pleasure still resided inside the codes.

When he rushed away from my shrinking apartment after twilight, Steve must have allowed his celebrity scrum to kiss away every dark worry that had attached itself to him. He had never wanted to dig out the errant cells with a potato peeler, or scrape away at his face until it stopped looking back at him with a dead man's stare. Instead, he was back on the Daytona beach, leaving the flounders and barnwallers behind. Head lifted up to the new sun. Fat waves rolling out in invitation.

Steve rustled past in his white suit, offering me a mango confection from the blender. He reached over heaps of old newspapers, piles of unanswered letters and an assortment of coloured gels donated for his next video. It would be structured like a lollipop, Steve assured me, shot in bright primary colours, its emotions swirling towards the top, sticky and sweet. We couldn't walk around in this place anymore, so instead we muscled our way through the waist-deep stacks piled high from one wall to the next. And always he was smiling. He just couldn't stop goddamn smiling.

Of course I worried he was in denial. Maybe he thought he had joined some kind of exclusive HIV club (which wasn't very exclusive), or that he had a right to win every argument now, his illness granting him a rare and never-ending moral superiority. *Of course I'm right. I'm dying, aren't I?* As long as he was still alive, he was getting away with something. Was that the story he told himself to keep the motors running so smooth? Why was he fucking smiling?

'Steve, I'm not sure how to say this exactly. I mean, I don't want to burst your bubble or anything.'

'You're afraid I'm too happy.'

'You sure look goddamn happy.'

'I feel goddamn happy.'

'You know this could be just a phase or something, right?'

'I love phases. I love knowing it's going to end, and that I'll be on to something else soon. It's like going on a holiday without having to visit an airport.'

There were no holidays from your own blood, I wanted to tell him but I didn't say that. I didn't say anything at all. Curiously, he was unafraid. He felt certain somehow that he wouldn't die of this disease. Which only made me feel worse, though I wasn't exactly sure why. All of the fear he refused found a home inside me. Someone had to take up the duty of all that worrying, and it was clear Steve didn't have the knack.

'You going to see Jody?'

'The guy who infected me, you mean? The doctor warned me against repeated exposure.'

'Funny word for love.'

'I just don't know that I'd trust myself alone with him, not now. Mostly I'd like to stick a fork in his face and turn him over until he's done.'

'Hard to imagine he didn't know.'

'A gun would have been quicker.'

'But that wouldn't have made him feel normal, uninfected.'

'The doctor said that because people are generally careful, because the word is out, infections are down to about one an hour. In other words … '

'You are not alone.'

'You ever wonder if all your friends slept with the same serial killer?'

Steve said he needed a few hours by himself and I didn't know whether that was such a hot idea, not now, so I held him very tight at his front door, more for my sake maybe than for his. I wanted to let him know, or let myself know, that it would be all right. I put on my game face, trying to absorb that small, lonely place of terror before it swallowed us both.

'Can I call you tomorrow?' I asked him.

'I'm counting on it,' he assured me.

It didn't happen all at once. I wasn't leaping over buildings in a single bound or anything, but slowly I was spending more time out of bed than inside it. I knew it was the drugs, my new body refashioned by science, the bitter orange swallows before meals, the large white tabs that tasted like teachers' chalk. Some stranger, some gang of white coats in a faraway lab had received a flash and now I was living inside it. Living.

My dreams were no longer filled with sexual Olympics, faceless giants filling international holes with combinations so beautiful that even the Russian judges cried. Instead, I had ordinary dreams filled with conversations about the weather. I dreamt about waiting for streetcars and watering gardens.

I got up and walked to the bathroom, which no longer felt like an endless and perilous journey. Cereals were poured and dutifully obeyed the laws of gravity. It was time. I gathered up the phone and called Cary, the man-boy who had taken my bottom-feeder perch.

'Auden? Is that really you?'

'Believe it. I know it's been too long, but I'm wondering if I can work my way back into the rotation over there.'

'Well, you're not going to believe this, but Johnson left.'

'He left the office?'

'Walked away from the whole company. He's doing a start-up on the coast, fresh accounts, the whole shtick. He wanted a change and cashed out.'

'But you're still holding it down?'

'I'm Johnson.'

'You're the cheese?' I asked him and I could hear him laughing in reply.

'Yes, I'm the cheese. So you want a reference or a job?'

'I want your job, Mr. Cheese. But I'll be happy with whatever.'

'Give me a couple of weeks and let me see what I can do. But in the meantime, Auden?'

'Yeah?'

'It would be good to see you again.'

Did I detect a minor note of romantic possibility? It had been a while since I'd made anyone laugh without having to plant my face in a doughnut. I pulled out the rumpled pad of notepaper and began transcribing our conversation, as closely as I could remember it. Steve had left with a caution that I needed to be extra-diligent now. We were nearly there, he told me, and even though I was feeling better and all, the machine was not quite together yet.

When the lines were laid up together in a book, they would form a trail that could be followed by even the most casual of readers. His idea, not mine. This trail might feel like a story, with its traditional entourage of beginnings and ends, and characters leaning towards resolution. They would long to close, just like the book that contained them. But the hope of the machine wasn't the delivery of great escape fantasies, instead it would settle a voice inside readers, steadily replacing the ones inside their heads with the ones that impelled the machine.

It was already happening to me.

I had jarred loose the voice that began with my own naming and that I had always felt certain would have the last word. The nattering list maker, the shaming baritone, the living Post-It note, the guilty party. All that dissolved as the new voice took hold. This welcome stranger wasn't busy asserting himself, talking all the time, like the old voice. Whole afternoons would drift past without a whisper. When I mixed up a shaker full of banana daiquiris the old voice would have looped cautionary tales, but the new voice didn't breathe a word of it. So instead of throwing the frothy confection past my mouth in hurried anticipation of the worst, I sipped it through *Buffy* reruns. I had guessed that the voice was a straight-up swap, but I was wrong on that count too. Without the anchor of my hectoring nag, the colours of my faded almost-sofa appeared like a Disney fantasia. I tasted each delicious moment before the next stood up to take its place. I could stand in the interminable lineups at the pharmacy without raising a hackle, perfectly content to listen to the fluorescent lights hum. I wasn't watching Steve's videos anymore, I was living inside them. Leaving the sickbed behind.

Steve and I made our way slowly along the dried-out riverbeds and uptown ravines until we arrived at the modest marquee that announced Maskerade, a legend among bars. Its success had been so phenomenal that where once lay a collection of flophouses so derelict even spray-painters refused to leave a mark, there now appeared an empire of buildings rising in a spray of steel and glass. Every kind of happiness was gathered here from around the world, which meant that locals never came, this was strictly for tourists. Not that we minded. On the contrary, ever since my diagnosis I'd become a tourist of my own life, and was still surprised how well that suited me.

I was steeled to deliver pep talks and affirmative actions along the way, but found myself hurrying to catch up with Steve's never-ending cheer as we strode too quickly north. I wasn't sure what was wrong with taking the subway, but Steve's new health kick (were those *muscles* I saw running between his shoulder blades?) meant that walking was the shortest distance between two points. What did he think, that he was going to live forever?

We stepped into a Maskerade welcoming mash-up of Mozart and the Bee Gees, some old-world orchestra swelling over the brothers' invocation to dance. A fiery runway parted the floor, and across its length paraded the main attraction, the handsomest men in the city. The manager, Eli Rooks, had personally scoured Toronto for his treasure, checking muscle mass and penis size, inspecting the teeth of young boys hopeful that one day they too might take their place in the soft arms of success. Once a master jeweller, Rooks had grown tired of the glass labyrinth he used to call home, and began to dream, in the diamond's thousand shattered reflections, of a new body that might return to its beholder something like a capacity for wonder.

It was rumoured that he saw well past the surface of his clients, noting the delicate join of muscle and bone and tissue that ensured a harmony of flesh, inside and out. And he had been patient. It had taken him the better part of a decade before he was satisfied, at last, that he had found the dozen young men who would come to represent an ideal not just of beauty but of truth.

The DJ shifted out of the Bee Gees into some moment of nineties devotion. Somehow, in this city's rush for the future, these old tunes had been left behind here in the mildewed juke-box of memory.

'I can never remember their names, the ones who did this song,' Steve told me.

'What song?'

'The song you're shouting over. "Groove Is Something Hard to Start."'

'"In the Heart."'

'Excuse me?'

'It's called "Groove Is in the Heart."'

Steve didn't sound entirely himself. And for that matter, neither did I. I worried we had been infected by some Gen-X nostalgia virus, but when I noticed a small grin tugging at Steve's normally imperturbable exterior, I realized that we were in the midst of yet another experiment. Of course, he had never let on. Somewhere between home and the bar we had managed to slip into someone else's personality, and I felt a flood of memories pushing out my own, foreign speech patterns occupying the place where my mouth used to be. Steve had broken out into a supersized grin. The sonofabitch. What if I got stuck, I wanted to ask him. What if these memories (was that really me running naked through the mall?) left permanent skid marks?

Steve, of course, only looked delighted, and that frightened me a little, in part because I'd never seen that much hilarity run around in his face. Knowing it was no use, I still couldn't help trying to hold on, even though the person I used to be was already overboard. Memories of a first kiss I never had, a painful-looking skiing accident and a bad break with family rushed through me. The muddier I became, the more Steve held on to 'Groove Is in the Heart,' a tune he not only remembered, but which was now the centrepiece of his new suburban personality. I looked down in horror to see that my foot was also keeping time with the beat while my pulse raced with an emotion that could only be named as joy. Ohmigod. I was enjoying this.

'Check out that chord progression,' he told me in a voice clipped from some bad teen magazine. This was really going to take some getting used to. 'The shine off those sampled congas, like you didn't have to sweat to make a sound so big. This tune came out when I was maybe fourteen, give or take a shave, a crucial fucking time for young ears, am I right? When you're fourteen you don't listen to these songs, you live them. So I saved my pennies and bought the record. They still had records then.'

'Vinyl changed lives, dude. CDS only package them,' I said, wondering where these words were coming from. I had been possessed by language, but I was starting to follow the tune. It was like watching myself on a game show.

'For two years this song was book and gospel,' the new Steve told me. 'I'm wondering what to wear and the tune up and tells me. Stuck for words? Just listen to that guitar solo. It's a big-ride feel for the mouth, it's a luxury fuckin' cruise with the top down and that's not wind pinning my hair back, it's love. I didn't know there was that much happiness in the world until they started the chorus.'

'Take a breath, honey, we're going to be here awhile,' I told him, my foot wearing double-time beats into the pressed linoleum.

'I stopped sleeping because there wasn't enough time in the day to write all the hit songs I was going to sing on top of the charts when I turned sixteen. Before I retired and began my second career as a surfer gigolo on Ibiza. So one night I'm running down the last instrumental break and then it was off to the boardwalk at four, maybe five in the morning. A lonely hour, a lonely time, right? So I caught up with this kid who was a pimple or two older than me, with a little pocket radio and it was actually in his pocket and that's fine, that's great, only he was playing *my* song. And he wasn't just playing my song, he was loving my song. He was singing my song. It's *his* fucking song now. I'm telling you, that's when I knew.'

'Knew what?'

'That personality was a virus. Everything I had was in that song, and then it was gone. He just took it right away from me. You don't follow, I can see that, but I had to start over. I mean, from nothing. I had to learn how to tie up my shoes and put milk on my Wheaties, the whole walk.'

'And being HIV-positive ... '

'Being positive is like seeing that little motherfucker with the radio in his pocket.'

'You don't have to sound so goddamn cheery about it.'

'There'll be different kinds of days.'

'I know.'

'But it's not always ... '

'No.'

'It doesn't have to be ... '

'Not at all.'

'The end.'

Steve was adjusting, changing speeds in his rumpled white paper suits, learning to say yes to being positive. He had company now, the reliable companion of his illness, and he brought it with him wherever he went, eager to talk all about it, to share in words what he could only dream of as a body.

And of course there were still the bad jokes he delighted in telling whenever he got the chance.

'What's black and white and red all over? A newspaper announcing my death.'

He decided to get up when he used to fall asleep, in order, he said, to have a look at the other side of his life. What he found there seemed to suit him well enough, because every time I saw him he held a distracted half-smile over his face, showing me, showing all of us, that even the very worst could be watered down, turned around even, in the simple act of embrace.

In the last few moments of Steve's epic serial project, *The Hundred Videos*, there was a palpable giddiness. As he approached the finishing line, exultation reached into that sonorous voice, dished up in the same endearing tones a child might use during a particularly glorious shit. I'M ALMOST FINISHED! He had proven himself capable of invention, his body helping to shape the world we live in. Next?

Wherever I looked I saw Steve's *The Hundred Videos*. They stared back at me from every ribbon cutting, restaurant christening and festival. Small, unobtrusive and always talking, they insinuated themselves into the life of the city, as if they were keys to understanding all that we could not, dared not, reveal to one another. They showed us what we were becoming. Documentaries of all that had not yet taken place.

'You remember what Cary Grant said?' Steve asked me, folding away headlines proclaiming his latest triumph.

'What's that?'

'"When I read about him in the paper, even I want to be Cary Grant."'

Soon, he confided, he would become unnamed again. He was already looking forward to it. But before he slipped away he wanted to weigh the overtures, wear the mask until he couldn't any longer. There were the predictable offers from MTV and the Sundance Channel, but the invitation that held the most promise was a request to work with students at Chicago's John Marshall Metropolitan High School. Marshall was a universe of basketball where students were expected to rub a few vowels together on their way to the cafeteria. Nobody made it to college from Marshall unless they could break down a full-court press.

Perhaps Steve's videos might offer a new look for kids that most systems had left for brain-dead.

I could feel the momentum gathering every time he brought it up. He was already tired of the art world's stretch for reputation and display antics. Here was the possibility of heading in a new direction entirely, where his work might be useful again. The pay was dismal, of course, but he had lived on less. Unspoken in these deliberations were my cocktail-inspired reanimations. My bed, for instance, was increasingly occupied only in the hours reserved for sleeping. Once-impossible tasks had become routine. He no longer needed to stop by each day, or any day at all, to see how I was doing. I was reluctant to admit it, in part because the consequences seemed so obvious. The better I felt, the further away he became. And though there were hours when my apartment once again became a hot white tunnel, these feelings grew increasingly rare, and I even came to miss the surges of fever, finding in them a last refuge, a final way of holding on to someone who had already left.

'Help me with this, would you?'

'Steve, what have you got in here?' I asked, lugging an oversized suitcase across the floor.

'It's my bricklaying kit. In case things don't work out at Marshall. You always need a fallback position.'

'I can't believe you're really going to Chicago.'

'Ditto. The best part about it is that I don't know anyone there. It'll be just like starting over. Hey, I think I feel a song coming on.'

Steve had chilled a little over the last few days. Not right down to catatonia and depression, but enough to keep him from jumping off balconies. He was letting the wind pass through him, this new feeling of being positive. At a time when I was a thumb-sucking approximation of a human being, curled up into my own fear, he was opening his arms wide, learning how to say yes in a new way.

'Karaoke is the only thing we've invented in the last century that really has anything to do with democracy. You think they'll have karaoke in Chicago?' Steve asked me, looking concerned, and I couldn't help wondering why. Was he planning on rejigging himself as a lounge act?

'Oh sure,' I let on.

'Well, they'd have to, wouldn't they? If you can't hum it or play a few bars it's not Chi-ca-go.'

There was nothing in his eyes that showed me today was different than any other day. Not yet. But I could feel the sadness bunching up in my chest, the conversations we weren't going to have, the things we wouldn't share any longer. The hope that things could stay the same. But they wouldn't. Geography would keep Steve and me apart until the two of us appeared like strangers, or, worse, we'd look at each other as something that might have been once but not anymore. That much was over now. It was over as soon as he decided to go to Chicago. As soon as he showed me how to begin this book machine.

Steve had granted me something like a new self, or at least hope. Wasn't that enough? But all of a sudden, watching his life disappear into boxes and suitcases, it didn't feel like enough. Not nearly. I choked back a sob and the need to wrap my arms around his throw-cushion thighs because those would be very un-Steve-like things to do. In fact, on the list of un-Steve-like acts, those would be close to the top of the list. Minutes passed and I was still doing my impersonation of a department-store manne-quin while he milled about his rapidly emptying apartment, humming and packing and sorting.

'Well, you know what you have to do now,' he said, fixing me in those soft blue eyes.

'I guess it's time to start putting together the notes, the writing.'

'The book.'

'The book, yes.'

'Just set it down exactly the way it happened. Or you could make it all up. The events don't really matter now, they're beside the point. You and I are beside the point. The only thing that matters now is the machine.'

'Yes.'

'I've shown you how the machine works, now you have to build your own.'

'Yes, but ... '

'You're worried about how it's all going to fit together.'

'I'm worried about you dying.'

I kept trying to have The Talk, reminisce about once-upon-a-times, maybe even toss in a bon-voyage fuck. Who knew how good we might be feeling by then? But Steve kept putting it all off, his last hours were filled with an almost manic urgency. I looked over to where he was stuffing his paper suits into a Samsonite clone, one after another, as if he would never find anything like them in Chicago, and maybe he wouldn't. Instead of saying another word about it, I bent down to help, folding and sorting and sealing book boxes shut with long stripes of clear tape. Looking after the details. Now there were only details between us.

When we were done, the last bin labelled, we stood by the window, and at last his face, which had been a frenzy of motion and concentration, was finally allowed to hit the pause button and let the mid-afternoon glare reach up over the promise of his mouth. I could see how tired he was all of a sudden as the rush of leaving caught up to him, to both of us. Without saying a word, he reached for my hand and held it in his own and squeezed very tight, his face unmoving, still staring at some beckoning moment in the distance, his future maybe, or mine. His fingers, newly bruised from packing, curled up into my palm. A bright yellow dot careened into the street a thousand miles below, and he looked at me then, the storm of Why You and How Many Times and Won't We Ever washed over him and then it was gone. I was already missing him.

'So give me a hug already, I see my taxi coming.'

'I can't believe this is really ... '

'Goodbye.'

'Goodbye, Steve.'

After all those years of watching movies, even my dreams were filled with title sequences and flashbacks. When I thought I was dying, I kept seeing a marquee with the words *Show Closing Final Weekend* flashing on it. And then one day the words stopped and I got better. It's funny because I didn't feel relieved or ecstatic. Mostly it was just disappointing, because it meant going on and it was getting easier not to. I started thinking of the 8,000 breakfasts that waited for me, or the nine months of my life I would spend brushing my teeth. How many times I'd have to stand with a big dopey grin on my face in place of conversation because all the words I once knew had flown south for the winter.

A thousand midnights before this one, when the dry coughs and night sweats were becoming reliable companions, my doctor asked, 'I'm not being alarmist, am I?' as he sent me off for chest X-rays that showed I had pneumonia. Again. I went home and lay in a small pool of my own sweat before Steve came over with flowers he'd picked from the police station. 'Government buildings,' he said, 'always have the best flowers.' But he turned black and white when he said it, as the fever slowly refurnished everything in the room.

There was a smell that attached itself to the dying, and I wondered whether it had started coming around. Jorge had it when the doctors made him day-to-day, but he charmed his way past that and actually left the hospital. No thank you to the wheelchair, he was determined to *walk*. But whenever I saw him there was this terrible smell that was worse somehow when he wasn't in the hospital because it was home there. When I went to see him in his steamy bachelorette it would hit me like a wall, and I'd want to back right out before getting any on me, knowing, of course, it was too late. I'd already got plenty on me, and my turn was coming right up. Soon it would be my friends hesitating at my door wishing they didn't have to come in, and for the most part, they didn't.

Please leave me alone to die. Just let me die, won't you? That's what I thought when he arrived, my Steve, lovely Steve, with a new concern and tender hands. It had been so long for tender, so long since I'd let myself anywhere near that. Not anymore, please don't remind me of that, it's just something else I'm going to have to wave goodbye to. But I felt him pulling me from the other end of the world, his world, reaching across the bodies that opened us like doors and left us unlocked, and the others, the ones who weren't around anymore, already past their last kiss, last word, will and testament. I could feel him reaching through all of them to find me on the other side, and I let it take me, the two of us, into something like normal, where the fever won't run into my lungs, and the illness can't follow. That's what his touch promised, that we had come too far, sung too long together, and that this feeling between us would provide shelter when the poultices and chicken bones and injections had failed. He held me in a soft touch, so soft it was hardly there, and made me promise not to leave. And I promised, I did. Knowing that I didn't own my own end anymore. That it was really a kind of last gift, the last thing I would be able to chip into the pot. I looked into Steve's eyes knowing that death wasn't final after all. I began to write.

Notes

While Steve Reinke is the author of *The Hundred Videos*, he is not HIV-positive! His good humour in allowing this project to wander from documentary to fiction is testament to a heart that is six times normal human size.

On page 75, 'I think it's true what they say ...' is from 'Love Letter to Doug,' #52 of *The Hundred Videos* by Steve Reinke.

On page 88, 'Like everyone else, I wanted to do something on AIDS' is from 'Excuse of the Real,' #1 of *The Hundred Videos*.

On page 91, 'The beauty of the world may be all around us, but sometimes it is hard to spot' is from 'Camouflage,' #96 of *The Hundred Videos*.

On pages 92–3, 'When my father died ... ' is from 'Joke (version one),' #13 of *The Hundred Videos*.

On page 104, 'Which gives the piggy bank more pleasure?' is from *Sad Disco Fantasia* by Steve Reinke.

On page 121, 'like a face drawn in the sand at the edge of the sea' is a quote from Michel Foucault's *The Order of Things: An Archaeology of the Human Sciences* (New York: Vintage Books, 1973).

Acknowledgments

For seeing the book that might have been waiting inside the alphabetic car crash, and for offering necessary vantages, this writing is indebted first of all to its editor, Alana Wilcox. Great thanks to video maestro Steve Reinke, who persistently sets the bar higher. And to the arts councils in this country who continue to make a home for small dreams.

About the Author

Mike Hoolboom is a Canadian artist working in film and video. He has made twenty films and videos, which have appeared in over 400 festivals, garnering 30 awards, including four in Oberhausen, a Golden Leopard at Locarno, and he has twice won the award for the best Canadian short at the Toronto International Film Festival. He has been granted two lifetime achievement awards, the first from the City of Toronto and the second from the Mediawave Festival in Hungary. He has enjoyed retrospectives of his work at the Images Festival (Toronto), Visions du Reel (Switzerland), Cork International Festival (Ireland), Cinema de Balie (Amsterdam), Mediawave Festival (Hungary), Impakt Festival (Holland), Vila do Conde Festival (Portugal), Jihlava Documentary Festival (Czech Republic), Stuttgarter Filmwinter (Germany), Musée des Beaux-Arts de Caen (France) and the Buenos Aires International Festival (Argentina).

He is a founding member of the Pleasure Dome screening collective and has worked as the artistic director of the Images Festival and as the experimental film co-ordinator at Canadian Filmmakers Distribution Centre. Since 2004, he has been working on Fringe Online (www.fringeonline.ca), a web project that makes available the archives of a number of Canadian media artists.

He is the author of *Plague Years, Inside the Pleasure Dome: Fringe Film in Canada* and *Practical Dreamers: Conversations with Movie Artists*. This is his first novel.

THE STEVE MACHINE 173

Typeset in Scala and Scala Sans.

Edited and designed by Alana Wilcox
Cover photo by Benny Nemerofsky-Ramsay

Coach House Books
401 Huron Street on bpNichol Lane
Toronto, Ontario M5S 2G5
Canada

416 979 2217
800 367 6360

mail@chbooks.com
www.chbooks.com